'It was after midnight when I got c Tammy. 'I wanted to look out of t I might feel better if I saw how normal everything was out there . . .'

'What happened?' said William. 'What did you see?'

'A creature,' said Tammy. 'Walking through the rain . . .'

It begins with an after-dark expedition to a local natural pool – Bablock Dip. But suddenly there is something moving round the village streets, dripping slime and weeds in its wake. Only Abi, Tammy, William and Isaac suspect the truth – but can they stop the monster before it grows too strong to be stopped?

The Thing in Bablock Dip is Rachel Dixon's fourth title to be published by Yearling Books.

THE THING IN BABLOCK DIP

RACHEL DIXON

YEARLING BOOKS

THE THING IN BABLOCK DIP
A YEARLING BOOK: 0 440 86327 9

First publication in Great Britain

PRINTING HISTORY
Yearling edition published 1994

Text copyright © 1994 by Rachel Dixon
Illustrations copyright © 1994 by Terry Oakes

The right of Rachel Dixon to be identified as the Author
of this work has been asserted in accordance with the
Copyright, Designs and Patents Act 1988.

Set in 14/16 pt Linotron Bembo by
Falcon Graphic Art Ltd.

Yearling Books are published by Transworld Publishers Ltd,
61-63 Uxbridge Road, Ealing, London W5 5SA,
in Australia by Transworld Publishers (Australia) Pty. Ltd,
15-25 Helles Avenue, Moorebank, NSW 2170,
and in New Zealand by Transworld Publishers (N.Z.) Ltd,
3 William Pickering Drive, Albany, Auckland.

Reproduced, printed and bound in Great Britain by
Cox & Wyman Ltd, Reading, Berks.

For Ellen

THE THING IN BABLOCK DIP

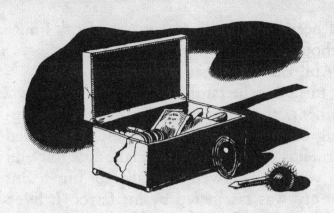

Chapter One

I walked up the narrow lane towards
Bablock Dip. Everything had gone wrong
and I needed to think. But the air was so
hot that it made my brain feel numb. Flies
hung over me in a relentless black cloud,
buzzing audaciously around my face and,
high above them, skylarks chirruped noisily.
It was impossible to concentrate.

And then I heard another sound from
behind me. A voice.

'Abi! Hey, Abi. Wait for me!'

It was Tammy Brown, my next-door
neighbour. We didn't really have much in
common, apart from our ages, but as usual it

had been impossible to get out of my house without her following me.

'Abi! Can you hear me?'

I turned, reluctantly. Tammy waved for a moment, then stopped, distracted by something in a field entrance. An old man called Cornelius lived there in a makeshift hut and we weren't allowed to talk to him. But Tammy was fascinated by his ferret. It lived in a cage constructed from an old shopping trolley, and I knew she would be making kissing noises at it for ages, so I carried on walking. Why should I make it easy for her to catch up? I didn't even like her.

I reached the gate at the end of the lane, but I couldn't get the thought out of my mind that Tammy might have disturbed Cornelius. He seemed harmless enough, but you could never be too careful. Trust Tammy to be so stupid. I'd have to wait now to make sure she was all right.

I climbed halfway up the gate and balanced myself against its rough wooden bars, but I couldn't see her. If she didn't turn up in a minute, I'd have to go back.

What a rotten summer this was turning

out to be. The main problem, the problem that was preying on my mind that morning, was Gran. While Mum and Dad were in Scotland, running an exhibition for their computer firm, she had agreed to come and look after me. But instead of taking me for outings and making my favourite teas, she seemed to be constantly tired and sometimes rather vague. So much so, that it was beginning to feel more as if I was looking after *her*.

I sat on the gate and felt in my pocket. There were three things in there. Gran had just given them to me and I still wasn't sure why. She had asked me to fetch her box of treasures from her suitcase. She knew I had liked looking in it ever since I was small and, for a moment, I thought she was going to pick out a trinket, to inspire one of her wonderful stories. But instead, she had pulled the battered lid off the box and said:

'I want you to have something, Abigail. Something to keep. Anything you like.'

I felt embarrassed. It was as if she was trying to make up for the fact that she no longer had the energy to do the sort of things grans ought to do.

'Go on,' she said. 'Take something. Each

item in this box is there for a reason. And each has its roots in this village. I'd still be living here, you know, if your gramp hadn't got his promotion to London. We used to live next door to the bakery, in the prettiest cottage you could imagine . . .'

I knew, of course. I'd heard it a hundred times, and loved it. But today, there was no life in Gran's voice, and no sparkle.

'I'm waiting,' she said.

I peered into the box. There were brass buttons in there, pine cones, little black and white photographs with their corners hanging off, bright marbles and cheap necklaces.

'I can't take anything,' I said. 'They're your memories.'

'Close your eyes,' she said. 'And take a lucky dip.'

It was a silly idea, but I closed my eyes, put in my hand, and took something. It was a stubby pencil, quite pretty but worthless.

'You gave that to me, when you were five,' she said. 'You bought it with your own pocket money.'

I felt guilty. Guilty for not remembering.

'Keep it,' she said. 'And take something else.'

I put the pencil in my pocket and felt again, this time right to the bottom. I drew out a small round seed-case, which I had never noticed before. It was about the size of a conker and fitted nicely into my palm. It was shiny black, but covered with green hairs that tickled my skin. When I squeezed hard, it felt slightly soft, as if it were made of rubber.

'You don't want to keep that old thing,' said Gran, holding out her hand for it.

'I don't mind,' I said, rolling it on my palm. 'It's pretty. And I bet there's a story behind it, isn't there? Otherwise you wouldn't have kept it.'

'Some stories are best left untold,' said Gran sharply. 'Now, put it away and try again. This time with your eyes open.'

I felt hurt and confused. Gran never talked to me like that. I quickly put the seed-pod in my pocket and looked into the box of treasures again. Lying in the centre of it was a brooch that should have been in Gran's jewellery box. Its amethyst stone gleamed amidst a delicate filigree of gold. I touched it for a moment, then drew my finger away. I couldn't possibly take something as beautiful as that.

'Have it, child,' said Gran wearily. 'If that's what you want, have it and enjoy it. You know it's of no use to me now.'

I took it and put it in my pocket.

But now, as I sat on the gate with the brooch on the palm of my hand, I felt so wretched I could have cried. It wasn't Gran's fault she was old and weary. And even if she had sensed my feelings and was trying to make it up to me, I shouldn't have taken the only thing of value from her box of worthless trinkets. The brooch belonged to her mother. It meant a great deal to her. And I knew I was going to have to try to give it back.

'Boo!' said a voice behind me.

It was Tammy. She had run through the fields to surprise me. She flopped down on to the parched ground. Her cheeks were fever red and her short hair stuck damply to her forehead.

'You've made me run,' she gasped. 'I've stung my leg on a nettle, I've been pursued by a plague of gnats, and now I'm going to lie down and die.'

'I shouldn't die there,' I said. 'You've got your head on an ants' nest.'

This wasn't actually true, but she sat up

immediately and shook herself vigorously, like a wet dog.

I couldn't help smiling, even though I was still cross with her for making me wait.

'Are we going to the Dip?' she said.

'I suppose so. There's nowhere else to go.'

'Have you got your swimsuit underneath?'

'No.'

'Neither have I, but at least we can paddle. That'll cool us off. And I've got two cans of lemonade in my bag, straight from the fridge.'

'Oh great,' I said. 'I'm dying of thirst.'

'I'll let you have some,' she said, looking me in the eye, 'if you show me what's in your hand.'

'There's nothing there,' I said. 'Nothing important.'

'Well it won't matter if you show me then,' she said.

'It's private.'

'No show, no drink,' said Tammy.

She was probably teasing, but I was too thirsty to argue. I slipped the brooch into my left hand and opened my right hand to reveal the pencil and the seed-case. Tammy stood up, to have a closer look.

'Gran gave them to me,' I said.

Tammy laughed.

'Is that all?' she said. 'I thought it must be the Crown Jewels the way you were going on.'

I opened my other hand.

'And this,' I said.

The brooch sparkled in the sun. I wanted Tammy to be impressed, jealous even. And she was.

'You lucky thing,' she said. 'I wish my gran was looking after me.'

'Well that just shows how stupid you are then, doesn't it?' I said. I slid off the gate and pushed past her, walking over to the opposite side of the field where a notice read:

PRIVATE
NO PUBLIC RIGHT OF WAY

Beyond it was a place where you could squeeze through a fence into Bablock Meadow. I pushed through and was irritated to see Tammy close behind me. We weren't really trespassing. Farmer Middleton knew villagers from Hampton End used this route to Bablock Dip. He left the sign up to discourage outsiders, who he much preferred to

16

use the public footpath skirting both the village and his land.

The sun beat down upon us, the flies still followed, and we could hardly find the energy to cross the meadow.

'It's too hot,' said Tammy eventually. 'I can't stand it. Shall we have the drinks now?'

'Let's wait until we get to the Dip,' I said. 'At least there's a bit of shade there.'

We trudged on.

'What's up with your gran then?' she said. 'I thought you were looking forward to having her to stay.'

'I was,' I said, 'but she's different. She's older and vaguer and she doesn't seem to have so much time for me as she used to.'

'I still think you're lucky,' said Tammy. 'Anything's better than spending the summer with a mum like mine. I thought she'd get off my back now there is no homework to nag about. But she always wants to know *everything*. She wants to know where I'm going, who I'll be with, how much I'll spend and what time I'll be back. She's so bad, I wouldn't be surprised if she asked me when I was next thinking of breathing.'

We reached Bablock Brook and walked

downstream beside its sluggish waters where butterflies danced amongst the tangle of scented balsam that crowded down to the edge.

Round a bend was the pillbox, a hexagonal concrete tower with narrow peepholes at the top. I had never liked it. It seemed ugly and out of place in the middle of the meadow. You could get into it through a narrow door on the brook side but there was nothing in there apart from rubbish and a bad smell.

As we walked past it we heard a moaning sound.

'Oooh, Abi,' said a ghostly voice. 'Oooh, Tammy.'

It was coming through one of the peepholes and we both recognized the voice at once.

'Get lost, Isaac Pottinger,' said Tammy. 'We know you're in there.'

'Prepare to meet your *doom*,' said the voice.

'No wonder it smells so much in there,' said Tammy loudly.

'Ignore him,' I whispered. 'He'll only follow us if we encourage him.'

'That's true,' said Tammy, quickening her pace. 'And I'm not sharing my lemonade with *him*.'

'Lemonade?' said the voice. 'Brill!'

Isaac darted out of the pillbox and caught up with us easily. It was no good trying to ignore him so we turned to face him. He stopped and stood confidently before us, slicking back his dark hair. He wore neat swimming shorts, flip-flops and an enviable suntan, and obviously thought he was Mr Cool.

'May I have the pleasure of accompanying you to the Dip?' he said.

'Get lost, Isaac,' said Tammy. 'You really fancy yourself, don't you?'

'Not as much as I fancy your lemonade,' said Isaac.

'Well you're not having any,' said Tammy.

'Want to bet?' said Isaac.

He snatched Tammy's bag from her shoulder, ripped open the Velcro fastening and pulled out a can of lemonade. Tammy flew at him, kicking and scratching, but he held the tin well up out of her reach. I managed to grab the bag from his other hand and thwacked him about the head and shoulders with it. But it was too hot to put any real energy into the attack and he eventually pushed Tammy to the ground.

'Thanks, Tammy,' he said, pulling the

ring off the top of the can. 'It's nicely chilled too.'

I considered rugby-tackling him but felt far too hot to bother. Tammy, however, scrambled to her feet and kicked him very hard on his ankle. He left, laughing, and it was only when he was out of sight behind the pillbox that Tammy allowed herself to rub her toe.

'He's got ankles like lampposts,' she said. 'I may never walk again.'

'He's a real twit sometimes,' I said. 'Couldn't he see we weren't in the mood?'

'Obviously not,' said Tammy. 'I expect he's worn his eyes out with looking at himself in the mirror.'

'He'll go too far one of these days,' I said. 'You see if he doesn't.'

Chapter Two

We followed the brook to the far corner of Bablock Meadow, where we stepped on to an arched stone bridge. Beneath us the water foamed its way over big stones into a huge pool. Surrounded by sloping grassy banks and with a floor of sand and pebbles, it provided a natural bathing area which deepened under the tall willow trees on the north bank to our right, but became very shallow beyond. On the far side of the pool, where the water was only ankle deep, a strong fence had been fixed to enclose it from the stream ahead.

This was the Dip, and it would have looked idyllic if others hadn't got there before us.

'Bother,' said Tammy. 'It's packed already.'

'It *is* the summer holiday,' I said. 'What did you expect?'

We stopped on the bridge and looked out across the water. On the south bank to our left, a large family lounged under pink parasols, keeping a watchful eye on their naked toddler who was paddling in the shallows. Where the water was knee-high, a boy floated in a huge rubber ring. And on the stones beneath us, two tattooed men in swimming trunks sat in the foaming waters. Their skin was a deep reddish-brown from too much sun and their paunches hung over the top of their elastic.

It was only as we walked to the opposite side of the bridge that we noticed William. He was sitting alone on the north bank beside a knotted rope that dangled from the sturdy branch of a willow tree.

He had moved into Hampton End a few weeks ago and did not seem to have made any friends yet – apart from me. I liked him; he was a good listener. And I had deliberately told him about the Dip in the hope that I might see him there. He had met Tammy and Isaac but I didn't think he had much time for them.

'Look, there's that new boy, William Carter,' said Tammy. 'You like him, don't you. Did you know he was going to be here?'

'Why should I? I don't live with him.'

'I bet you wish you did though,' said Tammy, grinning.

'Of course I don't.'

'Hi, William,' yelled Tammy, waving her arms. 'Over here!'

He looked towards us and smiled, but I had to pretend I wasn't with Tammy because everyone else was looking too.

'Let's go and share my lemonade with him,' said Tammy. 'And tell him about that pig, Isaac.'

We sat with William on the dried mud and shared the lemonade. Even in the shade, the heat was intense and we only had a few gulps each.

'That didn't go far,' said Tammy, draining the can. 'I'm going to have to drink the entire Dip.'

'No you're not,' said William. 'I've got

some Coke left.' He pulled a large plastic bottle out of a carrier bag.

'Oh, neat,' said Tammy, helping herself.

'How are you getting on with your gran, Abi?' said William.

'OK,' I said. 'But she's different . . . older, I suppose. And she gets a bit tired and muddled.'

'Is that a problem?'

'Not really,' I said. 'It's nothing I can't cope with, but . . .'

'But you wish things didn't have to change,' said William.

I nodded.

'I know how you feel,' he said. 'I wasn't keen on moving here. I liked things the way they were . . . but it's not as bad as I thought it would be.'

'And now, William,' said Tammy, putting the top back on the Coke bottle, 'I'll tell you all about rope drops.'

A little way out from the bank, the floor of the Dip sloped down into a bowl-shaped pool about two metres deep. The secret of doing a rope drop was to swing out as far as you could on the rope, then drop like a stone right into the centre of it. It was quite safe to jump there as long as you could swim. There were no jagged rocks or hidden currents – just clear water. And if the light was right you could see the sun gleaming on the pebbles at the bottom.

Tammy explained the procedure to William, with great enthusiasm.

'It sounds fun,' said William, looking up at the rope. 'But I don't think I'd be very good at landing where I wanted to. How do you manage to swing out far enough?'

'It's easy,' said Tammy. 'I'd give you a demonstration, only I haven't got my swimmers.'

'You could still show him how to run up and swing,' I said.

'I can't,' said Tammy. 'We've got visitors this afternoon and if I get muddy rope marks on this skirt my mum will kill me. You'll have to do it.'

'But I'm not as good as you,' I said.

'I bet you are,' said William.

'She's not,' said Tammy. 'But that's no reason for her to be chicken.'

'I'm *not* chicken,' I said, standing crossly. 'Just catch me when I swing back, that's all.'

I took hold of the rope, walked back up

the bank with it and pulled it taut. Then I ran down towards the water, jumping on to the knot with one foot on either side, as I pushed off from the bank. For once, my timing was perfect and the rope swung impressively out over the Dip so I was right above the deepest part. Tammy and William clapped and I was tempted to drop, just to show I could do it.

But I didn't. And after that things started to go wrong. My feet slipped off the knot and, in winding my legs around the rope to stop myself from falling, I somehow tipped myself upside down. I reached the bank with my long hair trailing all over the dried mud and my feet in the air. I could hear Tammy shrieking with laughter and realized that there was little chance of her catching me.

'Grab the rope, you idiot,' I yelled.

But it was too late and I swung awkwardly out over the water again. I must have looked really stupid but, worse than that, I felt something falling out of my shorts' pocket into the water. Tammy didn't notice. She was far too busy rolling about on the ground. I was sliding down the rope now and, if it hadn't have been for William, I would probably have ended up headfirst in the water. But as soon as the rope was within reach again he hauled me over the bank, where I fell to the ground in an undignified heap.

'I think something fell out of your pocket,' said William. 'Was it important?'

'I'm not sure,' I said, trying to do something with my hair. 'I had three things in there, but only one of them matters.'

I stood and felt in my pocket. Tammy, who had finally stopped laughing, sat up and I was pleased to notice a large mud stain on her skirt.

'You haven't gone and lost that brooch, have you?' she said.

The pocket was empty.

'Pull it inside out to make sure,' said Tammy.

'Don't be stupid,' I said, pulling out the pocket. 'I've lost it. And it's all your fault.'

'Wait a minute,' said William. 'There's something in the fold of the lining. Something shiny.'

It was the brooch, caught in the material by its pin. William carefully removed it and put it in my hand.

'See,' said Tammy. 'I told you.'

'It's beautiful, Abi,' said William. 'But I don't think you should be carrying it about with you.'

'I know,' I said. 'I'll put it somewhere safe when I get home.'

We all sat down and William handed me the Coke.

'So that was a demonstration of how *not* to do rope drops, was it?' he said. 'I wish I'd brought my mum's camcorder.'

'Oh, yes!' said Tammy. 'We could have sent the video to one of those telly programmes where they show people making idiots of themselves.'

I should have been cross, but William smiled so nicely at the idea that I couldn't help smiling back.

Tammy began to tell William an exaggerated version of the tale of Isaac and the can of lemonade and I let her get on with it. I leaned back against the willow tree, sipping Coke and, as I watched busy insects scurrying in and out of the cracks in the dry earth, I realized that this was the first time I had felt at peace for days.

'Hi!' said a voice. 'Save a bit for me, won't you, Abi?'

It was Isaac, yelling from the bridge.

'No chance,' shouted Tammy. She snatched the bottle rudely from me and had gulped down the last of the Coke before Isaac reached us.

'What did you have to do that for, Tamms?' he said, trying to look hurt. 'I'm still thirsty.'

'It's fair exchange for my lemonade,' said Tammy, grinning. 'So drop dead.'

'No way,' said Isaac. 'If anybody's going to die, it's you.'

'Oh, no!' said Tammy, cowering sarcastically. 'I'm terrified.'

Isaac picked up the plastic bottle from beside her and prodded her in the ribs with it until she flailed about, giggling. She grabbed hold of the bottle and, as they struggled, it flew out of her hands into the water and began to float slowly across the Dip.

'Now look what you've done,' said Isaac, standing. 'You've put litter in the Dip. I think you'd better get it out, don't you?' He began to shuffle her towards the edge.

'You started it,' said Tammy, wriggling away from him. 'So you can get it.'

'Go on, Isaac,' said William. 'You're the one with the swimmers on.'

I kept out of it; I knew it would only encourage them.

'You get it,' said Isaac. 'It's your bottle.'

'That's not the point,' said William.

'Scared of getting wet, are you?'

'Of course not.'

'No?' said Isaac. He took hold of the knotted rope that hung from the tree above us. 'Let's see you do a rope drop then.'

'No.'

The bottle was drifting across the Dip, gradually sinking as it filled with water, and it seemed there was no way either William or Isaac was going to give in.

'I thought you'd want to demonstrate how it's done, Isaac,' said Tammy, slyly. 'After all, William *is* new . . . he's only seen Abi's version of a rope drop. And you can imagine what *that* was like.'

'No wonder he's chicken,' said Isaac.

'I'm not chicken,' said William.

'I bet you can't pick up the bottle as you go under, Isaac,' said Tammy.

This was pretty clever of her. Of the three of us, Isaac was by far the most accomplished rope dropper and she knew he would be unable to resist the challenge. He stood up straight and looked coolly at each of us in turn.

'A bet, is it?' he said. 'Fine.'

He took hold of the rope and walked backwards until it was tight. The bottle had nearly disappeared under the surface.

'You'll never do it now,' said Tammy.

'If you're so sure of that,' said Isaac, 'you won't mind agreeing to *my* terms.'

'What terms?' said Tammy.

'If I do it,' said Isaac, 'each of *you* has to do a rope drop.'

'Easy peasy,' said Tammy. She looked at William and me. 'You'll have a go, won't you? I don't care now. We'll soon dry out in this heat and my skirt is filthy anyway.'

William and I exchanged glances. He grinned, and suddenly I didn't care either.

'Why not?' I said. 'I could do with cooling off. And I'm sure my gran won't notice what state my clothes are in.'

'OK,' said William. 'We'll all jump.'

Isaac gauged the distance carefully by eye, deftly pulled himself up on the rope and swung high over the Dip. It was a brilliant swing, the highest I had ever seen him do and, in that motionless second just before the rope swung back, he released his hold and dropped down towards the water. As he fell he curved his body into a graceful dive that allowed him to take the Coke bottle in his hand as he went under.

'He's good,' said William.

'Not bad,' said Tammy indifferently. But I could tell she was impressed.

Isaac swam underwater for a moment before surfacing. He waded to the edge, climbed agilely on to the bank and handed William the bottle without a word. He then slicked back his wet hair and sat on one of the tree roots in dignified silence.

'I suppose it's our turn then,' said Tammy, taking off her watch. 'Shall I go first?'

But Isaac smiled oddly. 'Oh, didn't I tell you?' he said. 'You don't have to do it this afternoon.' He looked round for effect. 'You have to do it after dark.'

'Don't be ridiculous,' I said. 'We can't come here at night . . . can we?'

'Why not?' said Isaac.

'It wouldn't be safe,' said Tammy.

'It's perfectly safe,' he said. 'It's been passed by the County Council as safe.'

'But not at night,' said Tammy. 'What if

someone got hurt? There'd be nobody around to help.'

'If we do agree,' said William, 'we'll have to have safety rules.'

'That's no problem,' said Isaac. 'You can go in one at a time, which leaves three others to make sure you're safe.'

'I vote we go ahead then,' I said. 'I'm totally fed up with this holiday. It's about time something interesting happened.'

'I'm in if Abi is,' said William. 'But we mustn't try anything fancy. Just straight rope drops.'

'I'm not sure if I can get out,' said Tammy. 'And he didn't *say* night before.'

'Too right, I didn't,' said Isaac. 'Because I knew you wouldn't agree.'

'What if it rains?' said Tammy desperately. 'It'll be too muddy to go in.'

'It won't rain,' said Isaac. 'But if you're so worried, we'll come to a deal, shall we? We'll come the first *fine* night from now. And, because it was my idea, I'll jump first. That way you'll know it's absolutely safe. I can't say fairer than that, can I?'

Chapter Three

Strangely, several rainy days were to follow with bouts of thunder and it wasn't until four nights later that we were able to meet.

The Dip looked different by night – wider somehow, and deeper. The afterglow of the sun cast a strange light, giving the trees sinister long shadows, and the air was heavy with huge moths. From beneath the big willow tree we could hear the water splashing over the rocks under the bridge and a lone bird called eerily from the opposite bank.

'I wish we hadn't come,' said Tammy nervously.

'It is a bit spooky,' I said. 'But nothing's

really changed since this morning. It's just dark, that's all.'

'Let's get on with it,' said William. 'Then we can all go home.'

'You're not scared, are you?' said Isaac, pretending he wasn't.

'Just get in there, will you,' I said. 'And as soon as you're out I'll follow.'

'I don't want to be last,' said Tammy.

'You go third then,' said William. 'I don't mind being last.'

Before Isaac started we switched off the torches he and Tammy had brought. He had wanted us all to drop in the dark and, if he was having second thoughts, he didn't show it. He stripped down to his swimming shorts, took hold of the rope, pulled it taut then swung easily into the air.

The rope creaked around the willow branch as he flew high over the Dip. He released his hold and we saw him drop down under the surface. Then there was silence, apart from the sound of ripples lapping against the grassy bank.

'Where is he?' said William. 'Do you think he's OK?'

An owl shrieked.

'He's staying under for as long as he can,' said Tammy. 'I knew he would.'

'Yes,' I said. 'He'll be trying to make his drop look better than ours.'

'But he may be hurt,' said William.

'Not *him*,' said Tammy. 'He'll suddenly appear on the opposite bank, laughing at us.'

William picked up Isaac's torch and moved it like a searchlight over the water but it reflected back off the surface, revealing nothing.

'Something's wrong,' he said.

There was an unusual edge to his voice and I began to feel uneasy.

'He must be out by now,' said Tammy. 'Nobody can hold their breath for that long.'

Suddenly Isaac broke the water's surface, threshing with his arms.

'Aargh!' he cried. 'My leg!'

'I might have known it would be a trick,' said Tammy. 'He's trying to scare us.'

'Very funny, Isaac,' I said. 'Now get out of the way so I can do my drop.'

'It's holding my leg!' said Isaac, who never did know when to stop.

He appeared to be pulled under now, his face contorted with fear.

'If it *is* an act,' said William grimly, 'it's a very good one.'

'It gives me the creeps,' said Tammy. 'He needn't think I'm going in there after this.'

But I'd seen Isaac's tricks too many times before.

'Don't be an idiot,' I said. 'You know what he's like. He'll come up laughing any second now.'

'Shut up, both of you,' said William. 'He's still under. I know he's always teasing you but I think this is for real.'

Isaac's head appeared again, in the shallower water near the bank, his mouth gasping for breath.

'My arms . . . get my arms!' he said, reaching out to us with desperate fingers.

'Quick!' said William, kneeling on the bank. 'One of you hold on to me while I grab him.'

Tammy froze, so I crouched behind William and put my arms tightly around his waist. He leaned out as far as he dared, gripped hold of Isaac's wrists and hauled him in.

Isaac lay on the mud, panting.

'Run!' he gasped. 'Get out of here.'

'You may as well stop fooling around, Isaac,' I said. 'We know you were just trying to scare us.'

'Yes,' said Tammy. 'We don't scare that easily.'

'I don't think he *was* fooling around,' said William. 'Not in the water anyway. It was cramp, wasn't it? Why not admit it, Isaac. It's nothing to be ashamed of.'

Isaac pulled himself up on to his knees and stared at each of us in turn. I wished he would stop it. His eyes were wide with fear, his limbs trembling. I had never seen him look like that before, and it made my flesh creep.

'Listen,' he whispered. 'I know you're not going to believe me, but there's an octopus or something in there. It wound round my leg so tightly that I thought I was never going to get up for air.'

'Stop whispering,' said Tammy. 'You're making me nervous.'

'There's nothing to be nervous about,' said William. 'Cramp can feel like that. I've had it.'

'It was waiting on the bottom,' said Isaac. 'It was slimy with weeds but it had a grip of iron.'

38

Water trickled down his face, but he didn't bother to wipe it off.

'Shut up,' said Tammy, her voice rising.

'It wasn't cramp,' said Isaac, standing. 'And I'm getting out of here.'

He pushed past us, limping away from the water towards the bridge.

'Hey, what about your clothes?' said William, gathering up Isaac's things. 'Aren't you going to put them on?'

'Leave them,' said Isaac. 'Leave everything. I'm getting out of here and, if you've any sense, you'll do the same.'

As we watched him stumble barefoot along the path we heard a noise from behind us. A sloshing of water as if something was in there.

'Quick!' cried William, dropping Isaac's things. 'Run for it.'

We all ran, stumbling along the path towards the bridge.

'Don't look back,' gasped Tammy. 'If it sees we're scared it'll be after us like a Rottweiler.'

'Just run,' said William. 'Run for your lives.'

I ran but, as we crossed the bridge, something made me turn my head. And across the

Dip, beside the knotted rope that hung from the willow tree, I thought I could see a shape dragging itself up out of the water.

Chapter Four

We didn't stop running until we got to the village memorial, where Bablock Lane met the main village street. Here, the bright lamps made everything feel more safe. And in the distance, a man was walking his dog.

We looked back along the lane and were relieved to see that there was nothing there.

'You've got to wait,' said Tammy, flopping on to the bench beside the memorial. 'I've got a terrible stitch and I just *can't* run any more.'

We didn't argue. My throat ached and my head pounded. I had never run so fast in my life. William bent over for a moment, panting, while Isaac stood a little way away from us, pretending to be completely unaffected.

'We've given it the slip,' said William. 'If there was anything.'

I saw Isaac cast a nervous glance back down the lane.

'I've left my towel there,' said Tammy. 'Mum'll kill me if she notices.'

'I shouldn't worry,' said William. 'Isaac's got to tell *his* mum why he's come home in his swimming shorts.'

'Didn't anybody bring my stuff?' said Isaac.

'I've got your torch,' I said.

'That's not going to cover much,' said Tammy.

She started giggling in a silly half-hysterical way. I wished she wouldn't. It was making me feel scared again.

'I don't know why *you're* laughing,' said Isaac, slicking back his damp hair. 'I won the bet, didn't I?'

'No, you didn't,' I said. 'You ran away before we could do our rope drops.'

'I didn't ask *you* to run,' said Isaac.

He was beginning to sound like his old self again.

'You *told* us to get out of there,' said

Tammy, wiping her eyes. 'You were scared silly . . . we all were.'

'Not me,' said Isaac.

He snatched his torch from my hand and left, limping across the village street in his damp swimming shorts with as much dignity as he could muster.

'It's time we all went home,' said William, looking down the lane again. 'But there's definitely nothing there. So let's go calmly. We don't want to attract attention.'

Tammy was trembling now, her teeth chattering, even though it was still very warm.

'Don't leave me, will you?' she said. She pulled William up to her on one side and me on the other. 'I need you both to walk me home.'

Tammy and I lived in adjoining semi-detached houses, just beyond the *Dog and Duck* pub. This wouldn't normally be a problem at that time of night but, as we approached the pub, we were surprised to hear music and laughter from inside.

'Shouldn't they be closed?' said Tammy. 'What if someone comes out? I'm dead if Mum finds out about this.'

'It's a Fancy Dress Evening,' I said. 'There's

43

a poster on the door. It says: *eight till midnight.*'

'It's only half past eleven,' said William, 'so we should be all right. If anyone comes out, just keep walking. That way they won't suspect anything.'

We reached Tammy's house without being seen. Lights were on downstairs and we could hear the drone of the television in the front room.

'You should be able to creep in without being heard,' whispered William. 'Good luck.'

Tammy ran to the door without a word, and stepped inside. But things weren't going to be so easy for me. My house was in darkness, apart from the hall light, but as I opened the garden gate I could see the unmistakeable shape of Gran moving past the frosted glass panel in the front door.

'You don't think she's going to the phone, do you?' said William. 'Perhaps she's discovered you're missing.'

'I hope not,' I said. 'She'll be going frantic. She might ring Mum and Dad . . . or the police. Do you think I should go straight in and tell her I'm all right?'

'I'm not sure,' said William. 'Did you expect her to be in bed?'

'Definitely,' I said. 'She said she was having an early night and I heard her come up before I left the house . . . but she does wander down to the kitchen sometimes, for a cup of tea.'

'There's no point in getting into trouble if that's all she's doing,' said William. 'Why don't you wait for a while and see if the light goes out?'

'All right,' I said. 'But let's walk on. It'll look less suspicious than hanging around.'

We walked on to the centre of the village. Here the main street passed between a row of shops on one side and the village pond on the other. There were six shop units in all, the first two of which – a general store with adjoining Post Office – were run by William's parents. Behind them, reached by a concrete drive, was a large brick-built warehouse which belonged to the shop.

At either end of the row of shops were concrete steps leading up to two-storey flats. The first of these, above the general store section, was empty with ugly FOR SALE signs pinned to its wall. But William and his parents lived in the second and we were pleased to see that all the curtains were closed.

We went over to the pond, stepping carefully over the duck mess and rejected bread crusts to the edge. The water was flat calm, gleaming in the street lighting and ducks, as still as decoys, slept on the wooded island in the centre.

'What happened back there?' said William eventually.

'I'm not sure.'

'Me, neither,' he said.

'Promise you won't laugh if I tell you something?' I said.

William nodded.

'When we were running over the bridge, I looked back,' I said. 'I don't know why. I couldn't help it. And it was probably my imagination, but I thought I saw something . . .'

'What sort of thing?'

'Just a shape really . . . dragging itself out of the water. But it nearly scared the life out of me.'

William didn't laugh. Neither did he look at me.

'I saw something too,' he said.

'Something big?'

'Yes.'

'I suppose it could have been a dog.'

'Yes, it could have been a dog,' said William. 'A big one.'

We walked up the narrow road that curved behind the pond to the last detached house in a row of four. This was Isaac's house. It was big and expensive-looking, with a garage, a carport and a bright floodlight in the front garden.

'It must have been difficult for him to get in without being seen,' said William.

'That's his room at the front,' I said. 'The one with all the posters. The light's on, so he must be in there.'

As I spoke, loud music began to play and Isaac appeared at his window, staring strangely out in the direction of Bablock Dip. When he eventually moved, something made him look in our direction and he opened the window.

'I've been grounded until further notice,' he said unhappily.

But before he had time to say any more, the music went off abruptly. There was some-one else in there and William and I ducked

47

promptly down behind the hedge so as not to be seen.

'Let's get out of here,' said William.

We worked our way well out of sight along the hedge, before walking back round the pond, in the direction of my house.

'Are *you* going to get into trouble?' I said.

William shook his head. 'I doubt it.'

'I hope Gran hasn't noticed I'm missing,' I said. 'She doesn't usually come into my room after she's said goodnight, so, with any luck, she's back in bed by now. I can't help feeling sorry for Isaac, though. I know it's his own fault for thinking of going down there at night, but we did all agree to it, didn't we?'

'You're right,' said William. 'We've got to be partly to blame.'

'Do you think it would help if we got his stuff?' I said.

'Probably,' said William. 'But I'm not going back there now, are you?'

By the time we reached my gate, a light breeze had blown up and the air was damp. Inside, the front hallway was in darkness. I was relieved, not only because it looked as though I was out of trouble, but also because I hated the idea of causing Gran any unnecessary worry.

'It looks as if we're in for more rain,' said William. 'And the pub will be emptying any minute, so you'd better get inside.'

'You don't think we ought to tell anyone about tonight, do you?' I said. 'In case there *was* something?'

'No,' said William firmly. 'Why get grounded for no reason? I'm creeping in as planned. We probably imagined it anyway. The dark can play funny tricks, you know.'

'Would you feel safe to go back there then?' I said. 'In the daylight?'

'Of course,' he said.

He only hesitated for a moment and I felt reassured by his display of confidence. But as I eased open my front door, I could hear his footsteps going faster and faster, until he was running like crazy for home.

Chapter Five

On Friday mornings I helped out at Hoskins' Garden Centre and Willow Bryan, who looked after the pet shop there, pulled up outside our house at eight-twenty. I was ready to leave, but as I ran down our front path I heard a voice from next door. It was Mrs Brown, Tammy's mum, standing in her dressing-gown and slippers, in their porch.

'Not so fast, young lady,' she said, beckoning me with a stern finger. 'I want a word with you.'

I walked reluctantly round to meet her.

'Our Tammy's been having nightmares, thanks to your little escapade last night,' she said. 'What have you got to say about *that*?'

What could I say?

'We woke up to her screams,' said Mrs Brown. 'She was as white as a sheet, poor lamb, scared out of her wits. She said she'd had a nightmare, but we got the truth out of her eventually.'

Trust Tammy to tell, I thought. The sneak.

'And next time you want an after-dark party,' said Mrs Brown, 'you'd better make sure it's properly organized, with adults present. You've scared her half to death with your spooky stories. She can't have had more than a few hours' sleep last night.'

'An after-dark party?'

'That's what I said,' said Mrs Brown. 'And you needn't start denying it, because I've got all the proof I need.'

An after-dark party was better than the truth. So I decided to go along with it.

'I'm sorry,' I said. 'It was a very silly thing to do.'

'Well you needn't bother calling for Tammy today. She's staying with me so I can keep an eye on her.'

'Will you be telling Gran?' I said.

Mrs Brown hesitated. 'Probably not,' she

said. 'She didn't seem herself when I spoke to her yesterday and, according to Tammy, you *were* only in the back garden. But I won't be so lenient if anything like this happens again.'

I wasn't sure if that was the answer I needed. I almost wished Gran *would* find out. Perhaps if she knew what I'd been doing last night, and not just Tammy's version, she'd realize she wasn't coping very well. Then, maybe, she'd ring Mum and Dad and get them to come home.

'Are you sure?' I said.

'Yes,' said Mrs Brown. 'Now clear off before I change my mind.'

I climbed into Willow's van, sitting with my feet amongst bags of hamster food and straw. Tammy wasn't the only one who'd had a bad night. I had spent hours going over what had happened at the Dip and now, though I had decided how I was going to cope with it, I felt relieved to be doing something normal and familiar. But instead of driving straight to Hoskins' Garden Centre, Willow took the van on into the centre of the village.

'I have a letter to post,' she said. 'Nip out and put it in the box, would you?'

It was as I stepped out of the van that we

saw William. He was standing, bewildered, in the doorway of the general store. And lying on the forecourt, amongst glittering shards of its glass, was the shop door, wrenched right off its hinges.

'They've had a break-in,' said Willow. 'And that poor boy looks as if he's had the shock of his life.'

'I know him,' I said. 'He's the son of the new owners. Please wait.'

I ran to William.

'Are you OK?' I said.

'I'm fine,' he said. 'But the shop's a right mess. Now the police have gone, we've got to try to clear up but with Mum in shock and Dad on the phone to a carpenter . . . I just don't know where to start.'

'Is it really bad?'

'Yes,' said William. 'Have a look at this.'

He led me inside and pointed in dismay at the floor where smashed ketchup bottles, broken eggs and yesterday's sliced bread lay like an uncooked breakfast. Beside this, in a pile of spilt salt, was an enormous stem of dried pond-weed and above it buckled shelving units slouched, smeared with foul-smelling green slime.

'It looks as if the crook came straight from the village pond,' I said. 'But what kind of person would do this?'

'Mum told the police she suspected that old chap, Cornelius, from down Bablock Lane,' said William. 'But I'm not sure it *was* a person. Not after what happened at the Dip.'

'About last night,' I said. 'I admit I was pretty scared and I was awake half the night. But now I've had time to think things over, I'm not so sure anything *did* happen. There wasn't anything definite to go on, apart from what Isaac said. And he's always been a great exaggerator. Things are bad enough for me without it, William. I'm really worried about Gran, for one thing. So can't we just forget it?'

'I'm sorry about your gran,' said William. 'But it's not that easy to forget. What about the thing we saw climbing out of the Dip? That was real enough, wasn't it?'

'It could have been a shadow,' I said. 'Isaac got us so worked up, we'd have made anything look like a creature. It's a pity he couldn't face up to the cramp, like anybody else, instead of going all dramatic on us.'

'I suppose you could be right about Isaac,' said William, 'but the state of this place can't be explained so easily. Do *you* know anybody who's strong enough to rip off a shop door?'

'Not really,' I said. 'But there could have been two people, or a gang, all pulling together.'

'OK,' said William. 'Supposing you're right, what would this gang have wanted to steal?'

'Cigarettes,' I said. 'Or drink?'

'That's what I thought,' said William.

'So what *did* they take?'

'Meat,' said William. 'They took raw meat . . . chicken legs, joints of beef, sausages . . . the lot.'

'Just meat?'

'Yes,' said William. 'So how do you explain that?'

Chapter Six

Hoskins' Garden Centre was at the end of a long drive that left the main street opposite Bablock Lane. It consisted of a large building with a walled yard beyond. The building was divided into various areas of interest, such as garden tools, lawn care and indoor plants. But Mr Hoskins was a poor manager and, apart from Willow's pet shop, the place had an air of neglect.

The pet shop was set in the corner of the main building with a door of its own. Willow liked it that way. Mr Hoskins was a very unpleasant man, so it was good to be able to shut her door when things got bad.

Inside the shop were hutches and cages with rabbits, guinea pigs, gerbils and hamsters. Three mornings a week, it was my job to clean them out. I also swept up and disinfected the floor. I had it off to such a fine art now that it didn't take long and any extra time I had, before Willow unlocked the door to the public, was spent with a very special rabbit called Currant. He had been at the pet shop for over a year now. He was black with a raggy ear and as he grew older it became less and less likely that anybody would buy him. Shoppers tended to go for the younger rabbits with perfect ears and I'm not sure Willow would have wanted to sell him anyway. She had even hinted that I might be able to have him if he was still unsold by the end of the holiday. I was sure he already thought of me as his owner. He came to me when I called, and would happily settle in my arms, letting me stroke his silky head for as long as I wanted.

I was still cuddling him when the main store opened that morning. Willow had nipped home to fetch some more bedding for the store, and I knew I could have a few extra minutes before she returned to open the shop, so I was annoyed to see Tammy peering through the glass panel of the door. Her eyes were puffy and she looked as if she hadn't had much sleep.

She tried the door handle.

'We're closed,' I said, stroking Currant's raggy ear.

'Please let me in,' she said.

'I can't,' I said. 'Not until Willow gets back.'

If she thought she was going to get a turn with Currant, after having the nerve to blame me for last night, she was mistaken. I turned my back on her and bundled Currant back into his hutch.

She rapped on the glass.

'I need to talk,' she said.

'If you want to apologize for telling tales to your mum, you can forget it,' I said. 'I'm not interested. And what are you doing out anyway? I thought you were grounded.'

'Mum's in here with me,' said Tammy, looking nervously over her shoulder. 'I was only allowed out because she wanted to return some secateurs. She's having a row with one of the assistants at the moment, but if she sees me talking to you, she'll go spare.'

'Tough,' I said.

Suddenly another face appeared beside hers. It was William and he had obviously been running.

'William!' I said. 'I didn't expect to see you here.'

'Mum and Dad sent me out,' he said. 'I was trying to help, but they said I was getting underfoot.'

'I saw what had happened to your shop,' said Tammy. 'Who do you think would do a thing like that?'

'I've got some ideas about that,' said William, 'but I can't tell you out here. Can you let us in, Abi, so we can talk in private?'

'Please do,' said Tammy. 'I have something to tell too. Something important.'

I unlocked the door reluctantly. I expected Tammy to make straight for Currant's hutch, but she seemed too nervous for that. Or guilty.

'You go first, William,' she said. 'Tell us about your shop.'

'I already know about it,' I said. 'And I don't think he should tell *you*. You can't keep a secret.'

'I can,' said Tammy.

'She can't, William,' I said. 'I wanted to warn you when I was at your shop earlier but Willow came in to get me before I had a chance.'

'Don't listen to her,' said Tammy. 'She doesn't understand.'

'What is there to understand about someone who tells tales?'

'I don't tell tales,' said Tammy.

'She told her mum about last night,' I said.

'I had to,' said Tammy, 'but I didn't tell her everything.'

'She told her enough to get *me* into trouble,' I said. 'She said I had invited her to an after-dark party in the back garden and that I nearly scared her to death with spooky stories. Her mum was furious. She was waiting for me this morning, the minute I stepped out of the house.'

'What did you have to do that for, Tammy?' said William.

He was annoyed with her, and I was glad.

'You don't understand,' she said. 'It was an emergency. Something awful happened in the night. You've got to believe me. I know I shouldn't have blamed Abi, but I couldn't think straight. Just give me five minutes to explain and I *know* you'll forgive me.'

I looked at William, expecting him to back me up.

'I can see why you're upset, Abi,' he said. 'But don't you think we ought to give her a chance to explain?'

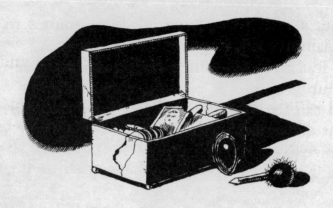

Chapter Seven

Before I had time to argue, Willow returned, so I led Tammy and William through the main building into the walled yard where I felt sure we wouldn't be disturbed.

It was a depressing place, square in shape with a heap of splitting compost bags stacked parallel to one wall. Manure and forest bark leaked out of them and there was even gritting salt, for clearing icy paths, that Mr Hoskins had failed to sell last winter. In the centre of the yard were the remains of a pergola. The climbing plants that had trailed over it had long since died and the flower-bed beneath it contained only an upturned water-butt and a balding yard-brush.

We sat against the compost bags.

'So what's the story, Tammy?' said William.

I turned my back on her. This wasn't my idea and I had no intention of forgiving her. She shouldn't have told tales about me last night. And she shouldn't have tried to turn William against me.

'They didn't hear me creeping in last night,' said Tammy. 'So I went straight to bed. But I couldn't sleep. I was too scared. I kept thinking about what might have happened if we hadn't got Isaac out of the Dip, and every time I shut my eyes I imagined octopuses coming to get me.'

'What sort of excuse is that?' I said. 'You've done nothing but follow me about this summer, yet the minute things get rough it's *me* who gets the blame. You make me sick.'

Tammy's eyes filled with tears. She's always been able to switch them on like a tap.

'Let her finish, Abi,' said William.

I knew he thought I was being unkind, but I didn't care.

'It was after midnight when I got out

of bed,' said Tammy. 'I wanted to look out of the window. I thought I might feel better if I saw how normal everything was out there . . .'

'What happened?' asked William. 'What did you see?'

'A creature,' said Tammy. 'Walking through the rain.'

Her voice was almost a whisper now and she held her hands together in a tight white knot.

'What did it look like?' said William.

'Big.'

'Was it a dog?'

'No. Dogs don't come *that* big.'

'What then?'

'It moved slowly on two legs . . . and where its arms should be, it had two long tentacles that stretched out like snakes. It turned its head towards me . . . and all I could see was an enormous mouth . . .'

'Where did it come from?' said William. 'Which direction?'

'Bablock Lane.'

'And where did it go?'

'I don't know,' said Tammy. 'I was too scared to watch. I ran back to my bed and hid

under my bedclothes, screaming and screaming until Mum and Dad came. I told them
what I'd seen but they wouldn't listen. They
didn't even look out of the window. Then I
said Abi's name . . . I don't know why . . .
to make them take notice, I suppose . . . and
somehow I mentioned being out at night.
I knew it was a mistake straight away, so I
made up a story about an after-dark party
at the bottom of our garden. After that they
decided I'd had a bad dream and that it was all
Abi's fault . . . and I almost believed them.'

'I suppose it *could* have been a dream,' said
William.

'No,' said Tammy. 'We disturbed something bad at the Dip last night, something
that terrified Isaac. I saw it, William. It was
in the village, in our street. It's already tried
to get one of us . . . so who's next?'

Chapter Eight

William stared at Tammy, his face pale, and I realized that he was beginning to believe her.

'It must have been a dream,' I said. 'Everybody knows creatures like that don't exist.'

'But I saw it,' said Tammy.

'She might have done, Abi,' said William. 'Isaac told us that something wound round his leg like an octopus tentacle. And you must remember what we thought we saw from the bridge.'

Of course I did.

'What did you see?' said Tammy.

'Nothing,' I said. 'And I bet you invented your creature to get sympathy.'

'I didn't make it up,' said Tammy, snuffling. 'I saw it. I know I did.'

'I believe her, Abi,' said William. 'Nobody would lie about something like that.'

I had to agree with him. And Tammy didn't look as if she was lying. But there must be a perfectly simple explanation. There had to be.

'I expect you've both forgotten there was a Fancy Dress Evening on at the pub,' I said. 'Suppose the "monster" Tammy saw was someone in costume, on his way home from the pub?'

'It was after pub closing time. I'd already heard everybody leaving,' said Tammy. 'And it wasn't a costume. It had tentacles . . . real, live ones.'

'Did it look like the sort of creature that could rip off a shop door?' said William. 'The sort of creature that would leave slime and weed all over the place?'

Tammy's eyes widened in horror.

'Is that what happened in your shop?' she said. 'I only saw the broken door.'

'Yes,' said William grimly. 'It wrecked everything . . . and all it wanted was meat.'

Tammy stood weakly, looking around her

as if she thought the creature might appear. My flesh began to creep. Something very scary had happened last night. It was getting hard to ignore but I knew I had to persuade them there was nothing in it. It was the only way I would be able to cope.

'Suppose,' I said. 'That someone *did* go to the Fancy Dress Evening dressed as a monster from the deep . . . they might easily have got weed and stuff out of the pond to make their costume look authentic. Then suppose they got drunk. They might have fallen asleep in the pub and left a bit later than everybody else. That would be when Tammy saw them. Drink can change a person's character, can't it? It can make them aggressive. It might even make them break into a shop . . . they might have wandered down there and smashed their way in. And as they wrecked the place, some of the weed might have fallen off their costume.'

'D'you think so?' said Tammy hopefully.

'No,' said William. 'Drink might make somebody violent, but there's no way it would make them want to steal raw meat.'

'Perhaps he was going to have a barbecue,' I said.

'You can't possibly believe that, Abi,' said William.

I felt myself blushing. Everything was going wrong. William was *my* friend, but now Tammy had got her claws into him, he was turning against me. He led Tammy gently back into the building. I couldn't bear to see him being so nice to her. I had to follow, to make sure she didn't say anything bad about me behind my back, but I needn't have worried for Mrs Brown spotted her straight away, gathered her up and left.

'Poor Tammy,' said William.

'Poor nothing,' I said. 'She deserves everything she gets, including her mother. And I think you were an idiot to tell her about the shop and the stolen meat. It was like saying you believed her stupid story.'

Before he had time to reply, Mr Hoskins stalked up to us.

'You kids,' he said, pointing nastily. 'If you're not buying, *get out*. I've had it with time-wasters.'

But as we turned to leave, we saw Cornelius entering the shop.

'That's odd,' said William. 'He's the last person you'd expect to see in a garden shop.'

'That's all I need . . . a bloomin' tramp in the shop,' said Mr Hoskins, waving his arms aggressively. 'Hey, you. Get out. I don't want your sort in here.'

Cornelius was not deterred by Mr Hoskins and he limped across the shop towards us. He looked dreadful. The whites of his eyes were pink, his skin unhealthy and his lank grey hair hung greasily over his collar.

'Has he got that mangy ferret with him?' said Mr Hoskins, stepping behind us for protection. 'Because if he has, I'll wring its ugly neck for it.'

'It's harmless,' said William. 'And for all you know Cornelius might want to buy something.'

'He can have some rat poison for his ferret,' said Mr Hoskins.

But, rather than leave, Cornelius stopped in front of us, swaying slightly, and spoke over our heads to Mr Hoskins.

'I'd like to borrow a spade, please,' he said.

'I beg your pardon?' said Mr Hoskins ominously.

'A spade,' said Cornelius. 'I'll bring it straight back. I wouldn't ask if it wasn't important . . . but something dreadful has happened.'

'You may certainly not borrow a spade,' said Mr Hoskins. 'This isn't a bloomin' tool library, you know. Besides, I know *your* type. Give the likes of you a spade and we'd never see you for dust. Not until you break into this place, that is. I wouldn't be surprised if it was you who wrecked the general store last night. Now clear off before I call the police.'

Cornelius staggered across the shop and slumped down into a swinging garden-lounger.

'That does it,' said Mr Hoskins. 'He's contaminating my garden furniture. I'll have to fumigate it. This is a matter for the police.'

'Good,' said William as Mr Hoskins stormed off to his office. 'Now we can have a word with Cornelius.'

'What do you want to do that for?' I said.

'I want to ask him a few questions,' said William.

'I'm not allowed to talk to him,' I said. 'And I don't think you should either.'

'Don't be ridiculous,' said William. 'He can't be dangerous in front of all these people, can he?'

'It depends what you ask him. You haven't changed your mind about the break-in, have you?'

'Not really,' said William. 'But I can't ignore the fact that so many people think it *was* him.'

He walked over to the lounger, and I followed. But Cornelius seemed quite oblivious of our presence.

'Excuse me,' said William.

Cornelius looked up, unhappily, and made as if to stand.

'No, don't go,' said William. 'I want to talk to you.'

'Well I don't want to talk,' said Cornelius, pulling at the frayed corner of his jacket. 'There's no point in living any more, so what's the point of talking?'

'Did you hear about the break-in at our shop last night?' said William.

Cornelius said nothing.

'Some people are saying it was you,' said William boldly. 'But I don't believe them.'

Cornelius narrowed his eyes suspiciously.

'It's true,' said William. 'I think you're innocent.'

'I don't steal,' said Cornelius. 'Never have, never will.'

'I believe you,' said William.

'I did have a drink last night. I won't deny it. But it wasn't stolen. You ask them at the off-licence. I bought it, with some cash I begged from a chap who was walking his dog in the lane. After that I spent the night in my hut. That's what I told the police this morning. And that's the truth.'

'What does your ferret eat?' said William. Cornelius looked up sharply.

'Now you're sounding like the police,' he said. 'Why is everybody so interested in Bessie all of a sudden?'

'Because it wasn't drink that was taken,' said William. 'It was meat. Raw meat.'

'You *do* think it was me,' said Cornelius. 'You're just like all the others.'

I tried to pull William away, fearing that Cornelius would lose his temper, but Cornelius seemed more unhappy than angry.

'Well, blame me if you like,' he said, 'but leave Bessie out of it . . . it's wrong to speak ill of the dead.'

'Dead?' said William.

'I should have gone to her in the night,' said Cornelius. 'But when she squealed, I ignored her. It must have been the drink that made me do it, but I knew I'd put the cover over her cage and I needed to sleep.'

'So what happened?' said William.

'When I got up this morning, her cage was wrecked . . . and beside it her little body . . . I didn't recognize it at first.'

'I'm sorry,' said William.

'She was the only friend I had,' said Cornelius. 'Poor Bessie.'

'So the police couldn't possibly have thought she'd eaten all that meat?' said William.

'Not once they'd seen the state of her,' said Cornelius. 'I don't know why they came really. I've never given them any trouble, not in all the years I've lived round here.'

He fumbled in his jacket pocket and pulled out a cheap flask.

'If that's alcohol in there,' said William, 'I don't think it will help very much.'

'Of course it won't help,' said Cornelius. 'I'd have been there when Bessie needed me if it hadn't have been for this stuff.'

He hurled the flask over his shoulder and it lodged in a plastic flowerpot, tipping a whole pile over on to the shop floor.

Unfortunately Mr Hoskins chose this moment to put his head round his office door.

'Hey, you!' he said. 'That's vandalism, that is. But the police are on their way and when they've finished with *you*, you'll think twice about ever showing your face in my store again. And just to make sure, I shall be off to the Dogs' Home tonight, to get a very big guard dog.'

And he slammed the door.

'All I wanted was a spade to bury my little Bessie,' said Cornelius. 'I owe it to her to do it properly . . . It was odd, the way that she went. Not what you'd expect . . . as if she'd been sucked dry. All that was left of her was skin and bones. But worst of all was the green stuff on her. Her remains were all slimy with it . . . I'm so glad I washed it off before the police arrived. I wouldn't have wanted anybody to see her like that.'

Chapter Nine

'Let's go,' I said, trying to pull William out of the Garden Centre.

I should have apologized to him. Somebody had to make the first move. But I still felt angry and somehow the words wouldn't come out.

'I'm not going anywhere until the police come,' said William. 'Cornelius needs a witness. He's done nothing wrong, and that's what I'm going to tell them.'

'You don't have to bother with an old man like me,' said Cornelius. 'I'm past caring now my Bessie's gone.'

'You're not going to mention *anything else*

to the police, are you, William?' I said.

'Only that I don't think Cornelius broke into our shop.'

I felt relieved. Telling the police about the Thing would be like saying it was all true.

'You're a good boy,' said Cornelius.

'But I'm going to see Isaac afterwards,' said William. 'There are a few questions I need to ask him.'

'I could wait and come with you, if you like,' I said.

William shrugged. I hated that shrug. It meant he didn't care whether I stayed or not. So I left.

I spent the rest of the morning brooding about Tammy and William, but that afternoon I offered to do the chores for Gran. She was feeling rather shaky and unwell, so I suggested she should rest for a while. The routine of dusting and vacuum cleaning was quite therapeutic and I got so involved that I forgot to feed Cleo, a cat belonging to one of Mum's friends. It was an easy enough job. The house was next door to Isaac's and all I had to do was dollop out a bit of Whiskas, mix it with a few cat biscuits, then freshen up Cleo's water bowl.

But by the time I remembered, it was dark. I left the house, determined not to be scared. I was tempted to ask Gran to come with me, but I could tell she wasn't well enough and told her not to worry about waiting up for me. But what if there *was* a Thing. What if it was out there? It was difficult to forget the look on Tammy's face as she had described it, but she might be watching from her house and I mustn't let her see that I was scared. I looked down the main street, this way and that. There was nothing about. I checked again, then ran swiftly and silently to the centre of the village, round the pond and up to Mollie's gate.

All I had to do now was feed the cat and get home. I could see the light in Isaac's window next door, and wondered if William had managed to speak to him that morning. If he had, Isaac probably hated me as much as William and Tammy did. If he hadn't, that probably meant Isaac was still grounded. So I put away any idea I might have had of ringing his doorbell and getting him to come with me, ran up Mollie's drive and let myself in.

Once inside, I was quite looking forward

to seeing Cleo. She was the sort of cat that made me feel special, and that was a feeling I could do with at the moment.

'Come on, Cleo,' I called.

I switched on the hall light and waited. Mollie always left an upstairs room open when she went away and Cleo liked to sleep on the bed up there.

'Come on,' I called. 'Wake up, puss.'

I went into the kitchen. Cleo's plate was empty. The poor thing must be starving. I rattled her biscuit box but she still didn't appear. She must be outside, hunting.

I pushed up the cat-flap with my foot and called. Cleo didn't come. I put out the light, pressed my face up against the patio door and tried to see her in the garden, but there was a big bush in the way, swaying oddly in the wind.

'Silly cat,' I said. 'I'm not hanging about all night.'

I felt disappointed that she hadn't come, but as I turned to switch on the light, I heard a scrabbling noise at the cat-flap. And I was aware of Cleo following me across the floor.

'There you are,' I said. 'I thought you'd left home.'

As I felt for the switch, Cleo brushed lightly against my leg. She always liked attention before her food.

'Just a minute,' I said. 'Then you can have a big cuddle.'

But something was wrong. Her fur was damp, her body clammy. In fact, it didn't feel like Cleo at all.

I found the switch, put on the light and turned apprehensively – to see a long worm-like thing snaking across the floor past my legs. I backed away from it, up to the wall, and stared at it in horror. It was covered with fur, like green weed, but beneath it was a black rubbery body that stretched disgustingly as it moved. And on the end of it a damp sucker moved this way and that. Searching.

I switched off the light, afraid it might have eyes to find me. And that's when I saw the rest of it, pressed against the rain-streaked patio door, foaming on to the glass from a huge mouth that squashed up against the glass, with two hungry lips like enormous slugs. It was the Thing Tammy had described, correct in every detail apart from its left tentacle, the injured stump of which thudded insistently against the glass.

I kept very still and very quiet, standing on tiptoe, so close to the wall that I could feel every knobble on my spine. But inside I was screaming. The door frame creaked. The window buckled. And I knew it wouldn't be long before the Thing burst in to get me.

But suddenly, from beside it, came a terrified screech from Cleo who had squeezed her way unsuspectingly through a hole in Mollie's fence. The Thing stopped pressing for a moment, its interest aroused by the tiny animal that cowered transfixed beside it. The long tentacle slithered back out of the cat-flap and, taking what might be my only chance of survival, and praying that Cleo would do the same, I ran like crazy for the front door.

Chapter Ten

Perhaps if Gran had been waiting up for me, I would have told her everything. I'd have had to. She would have seen the fear on my face. But when I got home, only the hall light was on and she had obviously gone to bed as I suggested. I stood alone on the doormat, weak with horror at what I had just seen, frightened that the Thing might be following me. I pushed down the Yale catch and fumbled the door chain into position.

But what if it came to the back of the house?

I ran to the kitchen, shot the bolts and double-checked the key.

'Is that you, Abi?' called Gran, sleepily.

'I didn't want to nod off until I heard you come in.'

My thoughts raced. Should I tell her? It would be lovely to feel her arms around me, reassuring me that everything would be all right, just as they used to do when I was small. But Gran seemed so frail at the moment that there was no telling what the shock might do to her.

'Can you come up, dear?' she called. 'I need to see you.'

I walked up the stairs, still not daring to speak in case it came out as a scream. I stopped outside Gran's room, put on a smile and stepped inside. She switched on her bedside lamp, blinking a little in its light. Her cheeks were strangely pink, as if she had a fever.

'Mrs Brown came to see me after you left,' she said.

'Oh?' I said, managing to keep my voice calm.

Mrs Brown had said she wasn't going to tell Gran about the after-dark party, but perhaps Tammy had told her some more lies.

'She brought me a few magazines,' said Gran.

'That's nice,' I said.

'But she also told me something very disturbing.'

Trust Tammy. The rat.

'She told me,' said Gran, sitting up uncomfortably, 'that something happened at the shop last night, something odd . . . and I was wondering if you had heard anything.'

'It was a break-in,' I said. 'But they've cleared it all up now.'

'Just a break-in?' said Gran.

She gave me a look that was almost knowing. I was feeling frightened and alone and suddenly part of me wanted to tell her everything. If only I could. Perhaps she would know what to do? She always had, in the past. But the moment passed. And Gran relaxed back on to her pillow before I had a chance to answer.

'I thought so,' she said. 'Lightning doesn't strike twice in the same place, does it?'

I agreed, puzzled.

'Just one more thing before you go,' said Gran. 'The gift I gave you . . . is it safe?'

She must mean the brooch.

'Of course, Gran,' I said. 'It's in my room. Do you want to see it?'

I knew I ought to give it back to her but I still hadn't worked out how to do so without seeming rude.

'No, dear,' she said, pulling the cool sheets up under her chin. 'But it's nice to know where it is.'

Chapter Eleven

I woke early on Saturday morning, stretched my arms above my head and traced my fingers around the bunches of flowers printed on the wallpaper. Through half-closed eyes, they didn't look like flowers. They were starfish, or ice-cream cones with dollops of different flavours . . . *or huge creatures with long tentacles and fur like green weed.*

I sat up, instantly alert. I was still dressed. The curtain beside my bed was open and rain streamed steadily down the window. I had been determined to stay awake all night. Watching. How could I have gone to sleep with a Thing out there?

I looked out of my window and across the garden. Everything looked the same as ever, but I knew the Thing could be anywhere in the village. Someone could even be dead by now. And it would all be my fault. I should have stayed at Mollie's and called the police. William was going to think I was a total idiot for letting it get away. But I knew I'd have to tell him. He was the only one I *could* tell now.

William was at our front gate within five minutes of my phone call, standing in the rain with water dripping off his anorak hood. I told him everything. I didn't apologize for yesterday and he didn't say, 'I told you so.' We just acted as if nothing had ever gone wrong between us. I suppose that's what you do with real friends.

'So what are we going to do now?' said William.

'Call the police?'

'But what if it's gone? They're never going to believe us, and we'll be in big trouble then.'

'We really need to get a look at Mollie's garden,' I said. 'But from a distance. If we knew it was still there, we *could* get help.'

'But how can we see in there?' said William. 'Without getting too close.'

'I don't know,' I said. 'Her garden has a huge fence all round it, with conifer trees along it.'

'It's a pity we can't get into Isaac's house,' said William. 'He knows about the Thing, *and* he lives right next door to where you saw it. We might be able to see something from his upstairs windows, but when I tried to talk to him yesterday his mum told me he was grounded until further notice.'

'Well I'm not going back into Mollie's garden,' I said.

William gave me an odd look.

'I don't think we have any choice,' he said, 'do you?'

Chapter Twelve

When we reached Mollie's front gate, we hesitated. We looked next door in the hope that Isaac might be at his window but his curtains were shut. In front of us, a drive led through Mollie's gloomy front garden, widening in front of the house to serve both a double garage on one side and a large wooden gate on the other.

But there was something wrong with the gate.

'It's hanging on one hinge,' said William. 'Was it like that last night?'

'I'm not sure,' I said. 'It was dark and I was in a hurry to get inside. But I know Mollie always locks it when she goes away.'

'It must be where the Thing got in,' said William, his voice unnaturally calm. 'Let's take a look.'

We walked up the drive, our feet slipping on wet moss. Conifers stood tall above us on either side, rain dripping steadily from their branches. I expected tentacles to reach out from them at any moment and, as we neared the gate, fear overwhelmed me. But William walked on, beckoning me to follow.

'I can't,' I whispered. 'I just can't.'

'We've got to,' said William. He took hold of my arm. 'Come on,' he said. 'We'll look through the crack to make sure the coast is clear, then once we're through we can inch our way along the side of the house. That way we can peep round the corner without being seen.'

Somehow we reached the corner and stood very still, listening.

'I can't hear anything,' said William.

He put his head round the corner but I couldn't bear to look. I braced myself, ready to scream, ready to run.

'It's all right, Abi,' said William. 'I think it's gone . . . it's left a bit of a mess though.'

We stepped out on to the paved patio. Set in

the centre of it, in the curve of a crescent-shaped rockery, was Mollie's pond, the only part of her garden she really bothered with now. Its strong mesh cover, put there to deter Cleo from fishing, had been ripped away and lay tangled beside it, crumpled as easily as a piece of paper. Dead fish floated in the muddied waters, their colours dim, and a trail of disgusting slime and sludge led over the pond edge, through the rockery and away across the patio. In it were waterlily roots, and tiny rock-plants, their leaves and petals crushed to pulp.

We drew up towards each other and stared down the garden, where the trail continued into a tousled clump of bushes.

'It could be in there,' I said. 'Watching us.'

'You're right,' said William, his nerve suddenly deserting him. 'Let's get out of here.'

And as we raced round the corner of the house, to safety, we saw a small sad corpse, green with slime, lying beneath a woody lavender hedge. Cleo.

Chapter Thirteen

Outside Mollie's front gate was a County Council van. It was parked awkwardly on the sloping alley behind the pond, its back doors open. A man in blue overalls was leaning inside and he turned sharply as we ran towards him.

'What do *you* want?' he said.

'Nothing,' I said, running past him.

I felt a little safer now we were out of Mollie's garden, but I had no intention of stopping. William, however, had other ideas and pulled me sharply to a halt.

'Yes we *do* want something,' he said breathlessly. 'We want help. A horrible creature has been in that garden back there. It's killed the cat my friend's meant to be looking after, it's wrecked the garden pond, and it could still be in there.'

'Well if that's upset you,' said the man, 'you'd better keep right away from my van.'

'Why?' I said. 'What's up?'

'If I'm not mistaken, your "horrible creature" was a fox,' he said. 'It'll have come from the fields behind the house. And a cat's not all it's had.'

'What d'you mean?' said William.

'It's had that lovely pair of swans out of the pond,' said the man. 'I've just picked them up off the island. And they're not a pretty sight, I can tell you.'

'Are you sure it was a fox?' said William. 'How could a fox have got to the island?'

'You'd be amazed where a fox can get,' said the man. 'But if it's any consolation, I doubt if it's feeling very well at the moment. There's something wrong with the pond.'

'What sort of thing?' I said.

'It's filling with slime,' said the man. 'Green stuff. You can see it in the deep water by the island. Some fish are dead already and one or two ducks seem to be sick.'

'Where could it have come from?' said William.

'I don't know,' said the man. 'I'll have to do some tests. But I'm not totally surprised, not after what's happened at Bablock Dip. The water there's got so filthy that old Farmer Middleton has had to fence the area off. He says it hasn't been that mucky since they stopped the factory upstream churning chemicals into the brook. And that was when he was a boy. It makes you wonder what's been coming down in the rain these last few days, doesn't it?'

'Suppose it didn't come down in the rain,' said William. 'Suppose it was caused by a creature . . . a meat-eating creature that goes for swans and cats.'

'You've been reading too many science fiction books,' said the man, shutting the van doors. 'You want to watch it or you'll scare that girlfriend of yours.'

'I'm already scared,' I said. 'Because I've seen it. It came out of the Dip the other day, it's been in the pond, and it's huge.'

'Sure it is,' said the man. 'And I'm the man from Mars.'

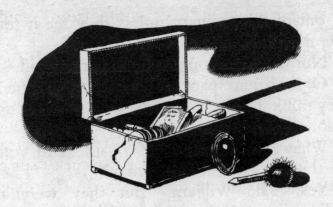

Chapter Fourteen

We went to William's flat to talk. I didn't feel nearly so frightened up there above the shops, but we positioned ourselves by his kitchen window so we had a clear view of the pond and the houses beyond.

'The man from the council has gone,' said William. 'I didn't really expect him to believe us, did you?'

'Not really.'

'So who *can* we tell?'

'Nobody, it seems. Not a grown-up anyway. Not until we've got real proof.'

'You're right,' said William. 'Grown-ups can't believe in anything the least bit weird or out-of-the-ordinary unless they see it for themselves, can they?'

'Not unless it's on the television,' I said.

'Or in a newspaper,' said William. 'Then they think it must be true, however ridiculous it sounds.'

'What about the police?' I said. 'Did you see them at Hoskins' yesterday?'

'Yes,' said William. 'But they weren't really interested in what had happened to Bessie. They just wanted Cornelius to leave without any fuss. I promised him I'd help to bury Bessie and that calmed him down enough for them to move him on.'

'And did you help him?'

'Yes,' said William grimly. 'I took Dad's spade down there. But I'm not sure if it made Cornelius feel any better.'

'What I don't understand,' I said, 'is how the Thing has managed to cause so much damage round the village without anybody else seeing it.'

'I know what you mean,' said William. 'But as far as we know you and Tammy are the only ones. It doesn't make sense, does it?'

'We both saw it after dark,' I said. 'Do you think that has something to do with it?'

'Perhaps it has to stay underwater during the day,' said William. 'But comes out to feed at night.'

'That would explain some of it,' I said.

'The weather's been bad too,' said William. 'So there haven't been as many people about in the evenings.'

'It has been in the Dip and the pond so far,' I said. 'And each one is turning foul.'

'Perhaps it can't stay in a place once it's messed it up,' said William.

'But if it's been going around the country polluting other ponds and streams,' I said, 'why haven't we heard about it?'

'I don't know,' said William. 'It must have come from somewhere. But let's worry about that later. It's far more important to find out where it is *now*.'

'It obviously had a look at Mollie's pond,' I said. 'But that's far too shallow.'

'Is there a deep enough pond round here?'

'Not that I know of,' I said. 'But there's the swimming pool in Isaac's garden.'

'You're joking,' said William, peering across towards Isaac's house. 'Why's the idiot so keen on leaping in the Dip all the time if he's got a pool?'

'It's out of order,' I said. 'Something to do with the filters. Besides, he much prefers to be somewhere where he can annoy other people.'

'Well the Thing should have found his pool. It's right next door to Mollie's,' said William. 'But surely we'd have heard by now. Isaac would have rung us, wouldn't he?'

'He may not have seen it,' I said. 'It's well down their garden with tall shrubs and things round it. And it's been so wet, I doubt if they've been near it for days.'

'So what do we do?' said William.

'Warn Isaac?'

'Not yet,' said William. 'Nobody will be in his garden in this rain and, if we're right about the Thing, it should stay there until dark.'

'Then what?'

'We catch it,' said William. 'Then they'll have to believe us, won't they?'

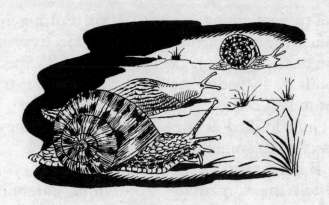

Chapter Fifteen

As soon as it began to get dark that night, I prepared to leave the house. Gran was sleeping in front of the television, and when she woke up, I hoped she'd assume I had gone to bed. I crept into the kitchen and eased open the fridge door. I was looking for meat. There were two pork chops in there, a packet of streaky bacon and some greasy cooked sausages. I took them out of their wrappings and slipped them into an old Sainsbury's bag but, as I turned to go, I saw Gran standing behind me. I wasn't sure how much she had seen so I tried to act normally, with the Sainsbury's bag held firmly behind my back.

'I'm just going over to Isaac Pottinger's house for the evening,' I said. 'He lives in one of those houses behind the pool. I expect you'll be in bed when I get back but I'll try not to wake you.'

Gran looked at me oddly, as if she knew I was up to something.

'Before you go,' she said, 'I want you to tell me something. And think carefully before you answer.'

'OK, Gran,' I said.

I could feel myself going red. And I knew the others would be waiting by now.

'You lost what I gave you, didn't you?' said Gran.

Was that all? She looked straight into my eyes, but I was able to return her stare with confidence.

'Your brooch is safe,' I said. 'I promise.'

'That's not what I asked,' said Gran.

'OK,' I said. 'I did lose it . . . but only for a minute. I was swinging over the Dip and I thought it had fallen in with the other things but luckily it caught in the lining of my pocket. I know I shouldn't have taken it out of the house and I quite understand if you'd like to have it back.'

I expected Gran to look angry or disappointed, but her expression was one of anxiety and confusion. I couldn't have felt more guilty if I *had* lost it.

'I don't think it pays to get some things wet . . .' she said.

'I'm really sorry, Gran,' I said.

But Gran was rambling now. And she didn't seem to hear me.

'Now the rain has come, hasn't it?' she said. 'Are the slugs out?'

'Lots of them,' I said, humouring her.

'Salt should do the trick,' she said. 'It dries them out. But you're a clever girl. You'll know what to do.'

'Don't you think you'd better sit down now?' I said, letting the Sainsbury's bag slide to the floor behind me. 'Let me walk you through to the sitting room before I go.'

I led her through and tucked her into her favourite chair.

'That's why it's been thundery,' she said, her eyes suddenly wide and alert. 'There'll be more. You'll see.'

Chapter Sixteen

William and I had arranged to meet outside
Isaac's house as near to nine o'clock as possible. I didn't like the idea of going over there
on my own, and was very relieved to see that
William was already there, if a little irritated
to find him already sharing an umbrella with
Tammy. I hadn't wanted to involve her at
all but William had felt we needed as many
people as possible if we were to succeed and,
apart from Isaac, she was the only other person we dared tell. She was leaning up close
to him, presumably whimpering about how
scared she was, and was all dolled up in an
embroidered white blouse, flouncy skirt and

frizzy hairstyle. When I got a little closer, I was pleased to see that her shoes were drenched and her white tights had a dirty tide-mark, just below the ankles.

'Don't you dare laugh, Abi,' she said. 'I know I look stupid, but William told my mum it was Isaac's birthday party. I knew it was an excuse to get me out of the house but I didn't dare argue over what to wear in case she changed her mind about letting me out.'

'I shouldn't worry,' I said. 'We've got more important things to think about. But don't expect a piece of cake and a balloon when we go home, will you?'

William gave me a look and I knew I shouldn't have said it, but I was feeling very edgy and I still hadn't forgiven her for getting me into trouble.

'I presume you persuaded Isaac's parents to let us see him.'

As I spoke, I glanced nervously into Mollie's garden but all was still apart from the rain.

'Better than that,' said William. 'They're out until late. He nearly hung up on me when I rang but I've persuaded him to give us a few minutes to explain why we need to see him.'

'Let's get in there then,' I said. 'It's getting a bit dark for my liking.'

'Me too,' said Tammy. 'I didn't really want to come out at night. But William persuaded me there was nothing to worry about. And I know he'll look after me.'

She smiled up at him, sickeningly.

William picked up two plastic carrier bags from the wet pavement and we set off up Isaac's drive.

'You got the meat then?' I whispered.

'We've done really well,' said William. 'I had to borrow some from the shop and I will have to pay them back somehow, but I told Tammy's mum any contributions towards a barbecue would be welcome and she's sent lots of hamburgers and chops . . . I don't know what we'll do with the chocolate dessert though.'

Tammy looked puzzled.

'Isaac obviously doesn't know we're bringing food,' she said. 'But that doesn't mean we can't eat it . . . and why are you both whispering? You're making me nervous. I saw something horrible the other night and you're making me think it's still out there.'

'You haven't told her, have you?' I said.

William looked embarrassed.

'You want him to tell me I was dreaming, don't you?' said Tammy crossly. 'I knew you'd turn him against me.'

'It's nothing like that,' said William. 'I promise.'

Tammy's face brightened.

'I get it,' she said. 'It's a surprise party . . . though why we should be nice to Isaac after he had the stupid idea of going down to the Dip at night, I don't know.'

William looked at me guiltily. He had got Tammy out under false pretences and we both knew it was too late to take her back.

Chapter Seventeen

Isaac opened the door promptly.

'I hope nobody saw you,' he said, pulling us inside. 'Because if my parents find out you've been here, I'm dead.'

'There's nobody about,' said William. 'It's too wet.'

Isaac shut the front door and led us to the kitchen. He wore faded denim jeans, cut off at the knees, and we could see a wide crepe bandage wound round his injured leg. I thought of the long tentacle that had stretched through Cleo's cat-flap and shuddered to think what might have happened to Isaac if we hadn't pulled him free. He was trying not to limp but I could tell it was really sore.

I was soon reminded that we weren't any safer indoors, for in Isaac's kitchen was a window not unlike the one in Mollie's house, the one the Thing had nearly cracked the night before. Rain lashed so hard against it that, in the half-light, it was difficult to see out. Anything could be on the other side. I strained my eyes and could just make out the tall shrubs that stood between the house and the pool . . . *if they were shrubs*.

'Mind if we sit down?' said William.

'I'm not sitting until somebody tells me what's going on,' said Tammy.

For once, she was right. William and I had agreed to break it to her and Isaac gently but now I wished he would just get on with it. They deserved to know what was out there.

William sat and pulled out a chair for Tammy.

'Abi and I need help,' he said. 'And you and Isaac are the only ones we can ask. The only ones we can trust.'

Tammy hesitated for a moment, then sat.

'It's about what happened at the Dip,' said William.

'I'm in enough trouble about that as it is, without having to bail you out,' said Isaac. 'I still haven't managed to come up with a convincing explanation for my parents and I'm grounded until I do.'

'We don't need that sort of help,' said William. 'We need to talk about what actually happened there.'

'Oh, I get it,' said Isaac unhappily. 'You've come to gloat. I just got tangled up in a bit of weed, that's all. And you needn't think you're going to get me to do a return dare.'

'We're not interested in dares,' said William. 'But we *are* interested in the truth. You were attacked, weren't you? It wasn't weed and it wasn't cramp. It was like you said in the first place. Something wound itself round your leg so tightly that you thought you weren't going to get up for air.'

Isaac looked hunted.

'I don't want to talk about it,' he said.

Lightning flashed and, almost immediately, thunder rattled overhead, making Tammy jump nervously.

'Scared of a bit of thunder, are you, wimp?' said Isaac, pretending it hadn't startled him too, teasing Tammy so he wouldn't have to face up to what William was saying.

'I am *not* a wimp,' said Tammy. 'You'd be nervous if you'd seen what I saw the other night.'

'Look in a mirror, did you?' said Isaac. 'No wonder you look so pale.'

'Shut up, Isaac,' said William. 'This is serious.'

'Actually, Isaac,' said Tammy, her voice almost a whisper, 'I saw the Thing that had hold of your leg in the Dip . . . and you wouldn't be fooling around if you knew what it was like.'

'Oh yeah?' said Isaac. 'What's it like then? The Loch Ness Monster?'

'It had two legs like tree-trunks,' said Tammy. 'And instead of arms, enormous tentacles, that reached right out towards me . . .'

A look of uncertainty flickered across Isaac's face.

'Good joke,' he said. 'You nearly had me convinced for a minute.'

'It's a killer, Isaac,' said William quietly. 'It's only had small animals so far: Cornelius' ferret, the cat next door and the pair of swans from the village pond. It's had raw meat too, from our shop, but it may not be long before it goes for a human being again. And that person may not be as lucky as you.'

Tammy whimpered a bit.

'Are you sure about all this, William?' said Isaac slowly. 'Have *you* seen it? Surely you're not going to go on Tammy's word?'

'He doesn't have to,' I said. 'Because I've seen it too. Last night.'

Tammy's mouth dropped open.

'It was next door when I went to feed Cleo,' I said. 'It has a vast black body . . . a cool damp body with fur on it, like green weed . . .'

Tammy hid her face in her hands and the thunder rumbled outside, but Isaac smiled strangely.

'I get it,' he said. 'You're so mad at me, for winning the dare the other night? You're trying to get your own back . . . aren't you?'

'We wouldn't waste our time,' said William.

'You're not kidding him, are you, Abi?' said Tammy, peeping out through her fingers. 'Because if you are, it's not at all funny.'

110

'It's true, Tammy,' I said. 'You were right about the Thing. And I'm just as scared as you are.'

'It's *all* true, Isaac,' said William. 'There *is* a Thing.'

'We think it spends the daytime under water,' I said. 'First it was in the Dip . . . the night it nearly got you. Then it was in the village pond.'

'But the water seems to start fouling up when it's been in there,' said William. 'So it has to move on . . . sleeping in the day and hunting at night.'

'Shut up,' said Isaac. 'I don't want to know.'

'We tried to tell a man from the council,' said William. 'And he didn't want to know either.'

'Nobody will believe us,' wailed Tammy.

'That's why we're going to trap it,' I said. 'That way they'll have to.'

'But it's huge,' said Tammy. 'How could we possibly catch it?'

'We're going to lay a trail,' I said. 'And the meat we've collected is for bait.'

'We thought we could start the trail before it wakes,' said William. 'Then as soon as we

111

see it coming, we can run ahead and open up the trap.'

'What trap?' said Tammy. 'We haven't got a trap.'

'We're going to use the big warehouse behind our shop,' said William. 'It's got thick walls and a tough metal door . . . and I've got the key.'

'I had a look at it this morning,' I said. 'And I think it will hold long enough for us to get help.'

'If this is all true,' said Isaac unhappily, 'why tell *me*? I'm the coward that ran away from the Dip. I'll be no good to you, will I?'

'We had to tell you,' said William grimly, 'because, without you, we can't get to where we think the Thing is hiding.'

Tammy stood slowly. Horrified.

'It's in his swimming pool, isn't it?' she said, backing out of the kitchen, towards the front door. 'That's why you wanted to come here. *It's in his pool!*'

'We're not sure,' I said. 'But it seems the obvious place, doesn't it?'

Isaac looked distraught.

'This is all my fault, isn't it?' he said. 'It was

me that made the dare, and me that disturbed the Thing.'

'It would probably have come out anyway,' said William.

'No,' said Isaac. 'I did it.'

He looked at us oddly. I'd seen that look before, when he was about to issue another dare, and right now it made me feel uneasy.

'So now it's up to me, isn't it?' he said. 'It's up to me to see if it's out there.'

And he opened the back door.

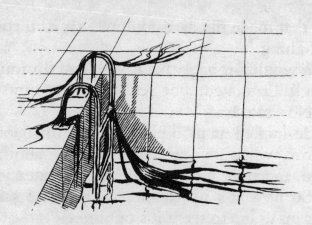

Chapter Eighteen

We felt a rush of warm damp air from outside. Thunder still rumbled in the distance but the rain had almost stopped.

'Don't be an idiot, Isaac,' said William. 'Nobody should go out there on their own. This needs careful planning.'

Isaac turned.

'Do you want to trap this Thing, or not?' he said.

His voice was calm, but I could tell from his eyes that he was just as scared as we were.

'Of course we do,' said William. 'But we're not letting you out there on your own.'

'You're right,' I said. 'We should stick together.'

'But what if we wake it up?' said Tammy.

Isaac hesitated, but refused to let himself lose his nerve.

'It's up to you,' he said. 'But I'm going now.'

He stepped out into the garden and we knew we had to follow. William and I went first, with Tammy close behind. We moved forward in a silent huddle, our shoes sinking into the sodden lawns but, in spite of his limp, Isaac was well ahead, and by the time we pushed through the tall shrubs he was already standing beside the rectangular pool.

'Get back, Isaac,' whispered William.

'Come away,' hissed Tammy. 'It's got tentacles.'

'You don't think I'd be standing here if it was in there, do you?' said Isaac, unable to hide the relief in his voice.

'Are you sure it's not there?' I said.

'Positive,' said Isaac. 'All there is is a bit of weed. Come and see for yourselves if you don't believe me.'

We walked down the sloping bank and joined Isaac at the edge.

The weed was green and lay in an enormous mass. There seemed to be no special shape or form to it and it was quite motionless beneath the surface.

'It looks harmless enough,' said William.

'It might not be weed,' said Tammy. 'The Thing was that colour . . . wasn't it, Abi?'

'She's right,' I said. 'I don't like the look of it.'

'Let's get out of here,' said Tammy.

'Don't worry about a bit of weed,' said Isaac. 'It's been full of weed all summer.'

And before we could stop him, he picked up a long-handled scoop that lay beside the pool and pushed it into the centre of the green mass. For a moment nothing happened. Then a long tentacle rose up like a vast glistening worm. Green fur lay flat against it, and at the end of it, was a sucker that moved sinuously this way and that as it sank slowly back into the water.

We stood in silence for a moment. Transfixed.

'It *is* in there!' said Isaac eventually.

'It's still asleep,' said William.

'Let's start the trail then,' said Isaac. 'I presume you lot brought the meat out with you.'

'We would have done if you hadn't rushed us out here,' said William.

'I'm not coming out again,' said Tammy, backing off up the slope.

'Don't worry,' said Isaac. 'There's plenty of time.'

But as he tried to pull the scoop out of the water, the mass of weed rolled slowly over to reveal two tiny eyes and an enormous gaping mouth, green with slime. The mouth closed hideously over the scoop, gripping it, sucking at it with an obscene grey tongue.

Tammy screamed.

Isaac's mouth opened too, wanting to scream, stretching tight until his lips were white. But no sound came.

Then the tentacles rose out of the water, winding round the scoop handle like a huge serpent, dragging it down into the water, pulling Isaac nearer and nearer to the edge.

'Run for it!' I said. 'Run!'

We ran up the slope after Tammy, slipping over the wet grass to the shrubs.

But Isaac was not with us.

We looked back to see him on the edge. Hypnotized.

'Let go, you idiot!' I cried.

'Come on!' cried William.

'Isaac!' screamed Tammy.

Lightning split the sky, thunder cracked overhead, and Isaac came round at last, releasing the scoop, yelling, sliding and jostling with the rest of us, running for his life.

Chapter Nineteen

It was only when we had closed the kitchen door behind us that we dared to look back down the garden.

'It's not following,' said William.

'Why have we stopped?' said Tammy. 'It can break down doors. Let's get out of here.'

'We've got to lay the trail like we planned,' said William. 'Otherwise it might wander off and the whole village could be in danger.'

'But that means somebody's got to go back out there,' said Tammy.

'It ought to be me,' said Isaac. 'It was my fault we didn't have the meat with us just now.'

'Why bother?' said Tammy. 'We know where it is. Why don't we get the police over here straight away?'

'I wish it was that simple,' said William, picking up a bag of meat. 'But even if they believe there's a creature in Isaac's pool, we can't guarantee it'll still be in there when they get here. It'll be on the loose and then they may not take it seriously until it's too late. Let's get it locked up, then ring.'

'I think Tammy's right for once, William,' I said. You've seen the size of it. I'm sorry, but I'm going to call the police while we know where it is. It's the only way.'

'Wait,' said Isaac, opening the door a crack. 'There's still no sign of it. I can run out with the bait and be back before you know it. That will cover us either way. I'll put meat from the pool out to the road. Then if it's out of the pool by the time they get here, it'll walk right out to the police cars.'

'Go on then,' I said. 'There's no time to argue. But hurry.'

Isaac boldly opened the door and set off down the garden but, before he had moved more than a dozen steps, we saw a large shape appear behind the tall shrubs.

Tammy let out a wail of pure terror that cut through the air like a blade. And, from beyond the meadow at the bottom of Isaac's garden, a dog howled in reply.

The Thing rose to its full height and forced its weight against the tall shrubs until their branches began to snap like tiny bones. Its tentacle reached through, then its vile head, turning from side to side, searching for us.

Chapter Twenty

Out beyond the meadow, the dog continued to howl in a crescendo of despair. Tammy was quiet now, with William's hand clamped firmly over her mouth, and the Thing hesitated, lolling disgustingly halfway through the tall shrubs. We kept still – very still – and absolutely silent, wishing we dared move to ease the door shut between us and it. The Thing was still too, listening. Then miraculously, it turned, crashing slowly back through the shrubs, trampling over bushes and flowerbeds towards the bottom of Isaac's garden where it forced its way through the fence into the meadow beyond.

It was only then that we dared speak.

'Now what?' said Isaac.

'We've lost it,' said William despairingly. 'And we've no idea where it's going.'

'I'd suggest we follow it,' said Isaac. 'But it's much bigger than I expected . . . and my leg's killing me.'

'We're lucky the dog attracted its attention,' I said. 'Otherwise we wouldn't have stood a chance. But why is a dog over there . . . and what's going to happen to it?'

'Hoskins got it from the Dogs' Home yesterday,' said William. 'Straight after Cornelius and the police left. I heard him telling Mum about it in the shop. It's not a proper guard dog or anything. It's just a young Alsatian that somebody abandoned when it got too big.'

'I wouldn't be surprised if he's tied it up,' I said.

'I hope not,' said Isaac. 'Or the Thing'll get it for sure.'

'Then it'll come back for us,' said Tammy, her eyes wide with fear.

'Maybe not,' said Isaac grimly. 'Not when it realizes there's so much food over there.'

'Food?' said Tammy.

'Pets' Corner,' said Isaac. 'It broke into William's shop, didn't it? So why should the Garden Centre be a problem?'

'It's live meat too,' said William. 'It probably prefers that to dead stuff.'

'But we can't let it get the dog *or* the animals,' I said. 'And worst of all, Currant's in there. I can't bear it if anything happens to him.'

William looked puzzled.

'Currant's a rabbit in the pet shop,' said Tammy. 'Abi's always cuddling him. Nobody else wants him, because he's got a raggy ear. And he's hers if nobody wants him by the end of the summer holiday.'

'I know he's only a rabbit with a raggy ear,' I said. 'But he's special. We've got to save him . . . *please*.'

And to my embarrassment, I felt a tear rolling down my cheek.

'Look, don't cry,' said William awkwardly. 'The Thing might be built like a dinosaur, but I bet we can still catch it if we put our minds to it.'

'Yeah,' said Isaac, trying to sound confident. 'We might be smaller than it is, but I bet we've got bigger brains. We'll save your rabbit and the other animals. No problem.'

'I'll help too,' said Tammy. 'If it means that much to you.'

And for once, I could have hugged her.

Chapter Twenty-One

We decided that two of us should follow the Thing and try to draw it back to the village, using the meat or ourselves to entice it, whilst the others tried to get help. Isaac's injury could easily hold him back, as could Tammy's silly party shoes. So William and I were the bait.

We ran to the bottom of Isaac's garden, the bags of meat flapping against our legs. We could just make out the shape of the Thing, moving slowly, about a third of the way up the meadow.

'Over here!' yelled William. 'We're over here.'

'Come on!' I shouted. 'Come and get us.'

But Hoskins' dog barked louder. And the Thing moved steadily on.

'I know a path up the side of the field,' I said. 'Let's get up to the top and meet it head on.'

'We can't do that,' said William. 'It'll corner us, like Mollie's cat.'

'Please,' I said. 'We've got to. I'm not letting it get Currant.'

I stood on Isaac's compost bin and clambered over the tall fence into the bottom of Mollie's garden. Here a loose panel led into a cultivated field which was separated from the meadow and the Thing by a thick hedge. I pushed through the panel and was relieved to see William behind me. We followed a narrow path which sloped up alongside the hedge. Mollie used the path often, but it was not accessible from the street. We ran up, splashing through muddy puddles, scraping against tall thistles, towards Hoskins' Garden Centre.

I reached the top first. Here the hedge met the wall of Hoskins' yard. There was a gap between hedge and wall, and I pushed my head through, looking nervously back towards Isaac's house. It was getting quite dark now, but lightning flickered in the distance and in its light I could make out a familiar clump of trees about halfway up the field. Above this was a large shape moving slowly up in the direction of the howling dog.

William caught up with me, gasping for air.

'Where is it?' he said, squeezing his head through, below mine.

'We've beaten it here,' I said. 'It's only just past that clump of trees.'

'I was afraid it would be quicker than that,' said William. 'We may still be in with a chance.'

As he spoke, the dog fell silent.

'What's happening?' I said.

'It's scented the Thing,' said William.

'The Thing has stopped moving too,' I said. 'Maybe it's more intelligent than we thought.'

'Let's start yelling again,' said William. 'We should be able to attract its attention now the dog has shut up.'

'It would be better if we could lead it down Hoskins' drive,' I said. 'We'd be taking it away from the pet shop and, if Tammy and Isaac have got in touch with the police, they'll come that way.'

'You realize we'll have to cross between the Thing and the dog to get there, don't you?' said William.

'Yes,' I said. 'But it's the only way.'

We pushed through into the field and, keeping close to the Garden Centre wall, moved swiftly across towards Hoskins' car park and the drive. There was no sign of movement from the Thing and I felt strangely light-headed, almost excited, as I realized we might actually succeed. But as we approached the car park, the dog began to bark again.

'It's heard us,' I said. 'Let's get out of here.'

'Ignore it,' said William. 'We're nearly there and it's bound to be tied up.'

'But the Thing isn't,' I said. 'What if it's started moving again?'

We peered down the meadow. I could still see the clump of bushes but it was even darker now and it was impossible to make out the Thing.

'Where is it?' said William. 'Where the heck is it?'

As he spoke, we heard a frantic scrabbling on the other side of the wall, and the dog appeared above us, growling fiercely, a length of frayed rope hanging from its collar. Its

fur was unhealthy, hanging limply over pro-
truding ribs and its eyes had the haunted look
of an animal mistreated.

We froze as the dog snarled threateningly.

'Keep your eyes on it,' said William evenly.
'And don't move.'

The dog stopped snarling and crouched
low as if it was preparing to spring. And
now it was still, we could hear the sound
of something else, dragging its way slowly
up the meadow behind us.

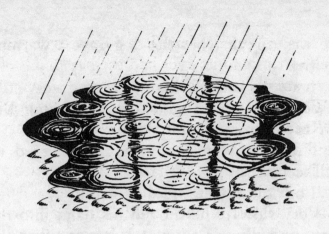

Chapter Twenty-Two

William reached carefully into his bag.

'It's all right, boy,' he said steadily. 'I've got something for you.'

He slid out a few sausages and slowly held them out towards the dog. The dog snapped them from William's fingers, with yellow teeth, and gobbled them down.

'Good boy,' said William, pulling his hand back quickly.

The dog relaxed its posture a little, obviously puzzled by the kindness in William's voice.

'Do you want some more?' said William.

He moved his hand towards the plastic bag

he was carrying but the dog gave a warning growl.

'It's OK,' said William, keeping very still. 'I bet you've been bullied, haven't you? But we're not going to hurt you.'

The dog whined a little and wagged its tail feebly.

'Poor old pooch,' said William.

Very slowly, he moved his hand into the bag, pulled out a chop and dropped it to the ground. Then he stepped quietly aside, not taking his eyes from the dog for a moment.

'Go on, boy,' he said. 'Try it.'

Lightning flashed and thunder rumbled. I jumped back, startled, and the dog tensed up again. It crouched on the wall, growling ominously. And we knew it was going to spring.

I dropped my bag of meat and ran, slithering frantically, to the gap where the hedge met Hoskins' wall. But William was not with me. I could hear him across the meadow, yelling deliberately to draw the dog away from me.

The storm erupted overhead. Extraordinary flashes of lightning ripped the sky apart, trailing each other round and round the meadow in a spectacular spiral. And in their light I saw that William was racing ahead of the dog, turning this way and that like a hare. In his hands were both bags of meat. He dropped one, then the other, but the dog ignored them, chasing after him towards Hoskins' drive. The dog was fast, but clearly unfit. And had it been a battle between the two of them, William might have stood a chance.

But watching from its position down the meadow was the Thing. It was still again, but the yelling, the sudden swift movement of the race, the terrifying power of the lightning and the roar of the thunder, seemed to awaken new energy in it. It raised its head, held out its huge tentacle to balance, and began to move purposefully and with sickening speed towards William and the dog.

'William,' I screamed. 'Look out!'

But the thunder drowned my voice, exploding on all sides, closing in on William, dog and Thing. William stopped, confused and terrified by the noise, crouching in a low tight ball of defeat. The dog reached him. But instead of attacking him, it sidled to his side and William, sensing its fear, drew it close to him where it accepted his reassuring arm like a puppy.

I watched helplessly as the Thing reached them and stood triumphantly above them, its tongue dripping with anticipation. It wrapped its tentacle tightly around William's wrist and pulled him away from the dog, lifting him effortlessly up into the air, where it held him for a moment, like a trophy, before drawing him towards its enormous mouth.

Chapter Twenty-Three

Just when I thought nothing could save
William, the dog began to bark loudly at the
Thing, leaping around its legs, distracting it
from its prize. Had the Thing not been dis-
abled, it could have dealt with William and the
dog at once. But without a second tentacle to
threaten it, the dog was able to close its jaws
around the Thing's leg, worrying and pulling
at it, until the Thing roared out in pain.

William, finding that the Thing had loosened its hold, twisted and pulled himself
free, slithering down its disgusting body,
scrabbling away from it and running across
the meadow towards me. He lay beside me,

exhausted and bruised. The sky glowed, strangely green, as the thunder and lightning began to dwindle. And out on the meadow the poor dog yelped thankfully as it reached the safety of Hoskins' drive.

Then the Thing turned towards us.

'It knows we're here,' I said, pulling William to his feet. 'But we'll never outrun it with you like this. We've got to hide.'

I dragged him back out of the meadow and along the wall to a pollarded willow tree.

'We're climbing over,' I said. 'Hoskins' yard is on the other side.'

'I can't do it,' he said weakly.

'Of course you can.'

I pushed him up, directing his feet into holes in the bark, placing his good hand on the wall and bundling him over into the yard. Then I hauled myself after him, grabbing young branches that could barely hold my weight in my desperation to get to the top. It was much harder than I expected and I had only just swung myself over into the yard, when I heard the snapping of twigs as the Thing pushed through the gap in the hedge.

I fell, not knowing where I would land.

A roll of springy plastic fencing broke my fall, tipping me face downwards into the dirt. I sat up and, in the dim light which gleamed through the garden shop doors, I could make out the pergola, empty fish-tanks and a litter of broken gnomes.

'William?'

I couldn't see him.

'Over here.'

The voice came from the opposite side of the yard, behind the bank of compost bags. I scrambled across and threw myself over.

'It's coming,' I mouthed. 'Don't move an inch.'

I hunched up beside him and waited. It was like a deadly game of hide-and-seek. I wanted to peep. I wanted to yell. But I knew I must keep absolutely still.

In front of me were the bags.

'Read them,' I thought. 'Keep calm.'

There was multi-purpose compost at the bottom, garden bark and horticultural grit, growing bags and 100% organic manure. And amongst them, in no special order, were numerous handipacks of gritting salt for icy paths with 'special clearance price' written on them.

Now what? I'd run out of names . . .
I must keep calm . . . There was rubbish
round my knees. How many different kinds?
I could see a lolly stick, a crisp wrapper and
a cigarette stub, a brick . . . and something
grey. A child's sock.

Then we heard it, the damp sound of
something moving in the field outside. And
a stone from the wall rattled down into the
yard. More stones fell, and more . . . and we
knew it was coming through.

The roll of fencing shivered, the gnomes
rattled and the Thing moved slowly across
the yard, closer and closer, until we could hear
it breathing on the other side of the bags. Its
tentacle slid over the top, groping with its evil
sucker, then an enormous head appeared, its
tiny eyes goggling, its grey tongue quivering
with triumph.

It had seen us.

Chapter Twenty-Four

I should have been terrified but, faced with the sickening knowledge that we were going to die, all I could feel was anger. I decided I wasn't going to go without a fight and I looked for something to throw, tugging furiously at one of the compost bags before me. It was far too heavy to lift but the bags above it wobbled ominously. Hoskins hadn't stacked them properly – rain had seeped between them – and I realized that they could topple over at any moment.

Oblivious of my feeble efforts, the Thing reached over the bank. It knew William was easy prey and curled its tentacle around his waist. William struggled to free himself but the tentacle merely drew tighter around him until he could hardly breathe.

'Run for it, Abi,' he said weakly. 'It'll get you next.'

'No,' I said. 'I'm not leaving you.'

I clambered halfway up the bank of bags, leaned against the top of the heap and pushed hard. At first nothing happened. My feet were slipping on the wet plastic and fear had sapped my strength. But the Thing was lifting William into the air now and I knew I had to try again. This time the bags did move, sliding heavily down on to the Thing's feet, showering its legs with a mixture of compost, garden bark and gritting salt. The Thing was startled for a moment, but not nearly enough to stop it.

'It's no good, Abi,' said William. 'Run while you have the chance.'

I began to wonder if William was right; perhaps I should try to get help. But as he was speaking, I noticed something strange. The Thing, which had been eagerly opening its mouth to devour William, suddenly drew sharply back across the yard, stepping out of the mess of garden materials in obvious distress. And I noticed with surprise that where the bags had landed, the flesh on its legs had begun to bubble as if eaten by acid.

'Look, William,' I said. 'Its legs are going funny.'

The Thing gurgled in pain, swaying from side to side and spewing green mucus from its mouth. It crumpled back against the pergola, splintering the wooden struts with its weight.

'Something's hurting it,' I said. 'Its leg's fizzling away.'

William struggled feebly to see, but the Thing seemed to be squeezing him harder than ever.

I looked at the mess of garden bark, compost and rock salt, I looked at the Thing's withered legs and suddenly I remembered the length of pond weed in William's shop . . . and echoing in my head were Gran's words . . .

'Are the slugs out? Salt should do the trick. It dries them out. But you're a clever girl. You'll know what to do.'

'It must be the gritting salt, William,' I said. 'It's drying it out like a slug. Don't you see? It lost its other tentacle in your shop. It was lying in a pile of salt on the floor.'

141

But William lay silent, slouched over the Thing's coiled tentacle.

I jumped down into the debris, stepping dangerously close to the Thing, and pulled out a bag of gritting salt. I tore at it with my fingers, and sprayed the contents up on to the creature's tentacle. It immediately weakened and sagged, and William slipped down from the loosened coil to the ground below. The Thing stepped back, confused with pain, moaning with distress as I sprayed on more and more salt until its tentacle finally dropped to the ground, completely severed.

We should have been safe now but, without its tentacle, the Thing seemed to feel no pain and it suddenly became aware of me, bringing its disgusting face down to mine. It was so close that I could feel its foul breath on my skin. I reached down blindly, took up a fistful of something, and threw it hard into the Thing's mouth. Thankfully it was salt and I watched with horror as its enormous head began to shrivel from within.

It was a terrible sight, but I thanked Hoskins for his inefficiency as I threw bag after bag, covering every inch of the Thing's head and body until it sagged down to the ground, writhing in more salt, drying out until all that was left was a heap of greenish weed with a mouth in the centre that opened one last time before it died.

Chapter Twenty-Five

William came round, gasping for air. He lifted his head and looked around the yard. Terrified.

'It's OK,' I said, running to him. 'It's dead.'

He pulled himself painfully into a sitting position.

'Shouldn't you lie down until help comes?' I said.

'Probably,' said William, propping himself against a bag of organic manure. 'I think it's cracked a few of my ribs.'

He looked in amazement at the green mess that had been the Thing.

'However did you manage that?' he said.

'It was the gritting salt,' I said. 'It dried it out like a slug . . . Its tentacle was fizzling away . . . it looked just like the length of weed you found, lying in a pile of salt on your shop floor . . .'

'You mean *that* was its other tentacle?'

'Yes . . . and then I remembered what Gran had said. She told me how to dry out a slug. She was trying to warn me.'

As I spoke, I became aware of a small figure watching me from the hole where the Thing had broken through. It was Gran. She wore her nightdress, dressing-gown and a very muddy pair of slippers. In her hands she clutched two large tubs of salt.

'It looks as though you managed without me,' she said breathlessly.

'Gran!' I said. 'However did you get here?'

'The same way you did,' said Gran briskly. 'Through the bottom of Mollie Pur-beck's garden . . . though I'm not so good at getting over fences as I used to be.'

She looked at William.

'You're hurt,' she said, stepping over the rubble towards him. 'Can you walk?'

'I'm not sure,' said William. 'I think it's my ribs. And my arm's badly bruised.'

'They'll have to bring an ambulance up Hoskins' drive and stretcher you over,' said Gran. 'I trust a certain rabbit is quite safe too?'

She sounded so much like her old self, that I could have cried.

'Currant is fine,' I said. 'And the other pets too. The Thing didn't get anywhere near them. There was a dog too. Hoskins had been cruel to it and now it's on the loose.'

'Don't worry,' said Gran. 'We'll get the R.S.P.C.A. on to it.'

'But how do you know about them?' I said. 'And how did you know where to find us?'

'I rang your friend Isaac Pottinger,' she said. 'The line was very crackly, but I could tell he was agitated about something. He was just explaining that he wanted me to get off the line when the phone went dead . . . something to do with the lightning, I suppose. So there was nothing for it but to hurry round there.'

I drew her towards some compost bags and sat her down.

'I met him in the street with that silly girl Tammy,' she said. 'And I wouldn't let them go until they told me everything. The poor things were desperate for help. I had rung them just as they were about to ring the police and I must have seemed a very poor substitute.'

'So where are they?' I said. 'And why did they let you come here on your own?'

'I sent them to find a working telephone,' said Gran. 'There must be one somewhere in the village. And told them I was coming after you. They tried to warn me off but I was so afraid you wouldn't know what to do that I had to come.'

'I don't know how you made it,' I said. 'You've been so . . .'

'Feeble?'

'Something like that,' I said.

'I feel so guilty,' she said, pulling her dressing-gown tightly around her. 'I've always been so fit. But I had a nasty virus, just before your parents left. I thought I was better, but it came over me again these last few days and I haven't been able to shake it off until now. I should have told your parents, I know, but I didn't want to let them down.'

'I didn't realize how bad you felt at first,' I said. 'I just knew you didn't seem like my gran any more.'

'If I hadn't felt so weary and muddled I could have dealt with this whole matter sooner,' said Gran. 'All the signs were there . . . but somehow I couldn't get my mind around them . . . not until some time after you left tonight. I think it was the storm that did it. It sparked off memories of things I had tried to forget.'

'Well you needn't worry any more,' I said. 'The Thing is dead.'

'So I see,' she said. 'Though I can't for the life of me imagine how you managed it.'

'There was gritting salt here,' I said. 'Lots of it . . . otherwise you might have been too late.'

William listened incredulously to our conversation.

'I don't understand,' he said. 'I thought nobody knew about the Thing except the four of us.'

'The Thing wouldn't have been here at all if it hadn't been for my foolishness,' said Gran. 'I feel responsible for putting you all in danger.'

'I don't see how it could possibly be your fault,' said William.

'No, dear,' said Gran. 'I don't suppose you do.'

During our conversation, Tammy and Isaac appeared at the hole in the wall, staring nervously beyond the rubble to the mess that had been the Thing.

'It's all right,' said Gran. 'It's quite dead, thanks to my Abi. And this young man is all right apart from a few cracked ribs.'

'Are the police coming?' said William.

'Yes,' said Isaac, exchanging a glance with Tammy. 'But there *was* a bit of a problem.'

'Yes?' said Gran.

'I rang them,' said Isaac. 'And told them about the Thing . . . but I could tell they didn't believe me.'

'So I rang back a few minutes later,' said Tammy. 'And said I'd seen a batty old lady in a dressing-gown wandering across the field towards Hoskins' Garden Centre.'

'And?' said Gran, her face a mask.

'They said they'd send a car over.'

'Pity,' said Gran, smiling. 'We don't really need them here now . . . and it will do nothing for my reputation.'

'But what puzzles me,' said Isaac, 'is how you knew about all this in the first place. I thought none of us had told anybody.'

'I knew,' said Gran, 'because this is not the first time the Thing has appeared. I used to go to the Dip with my friend Edith from the bakery when I was about your age. You won't know the bakery . . . it's gone now. But the Dip is still there. Nobody else went there in those days; it was too badly polluted with scum and slime from the chemical factory up the stream. But one night we went there for a dare . . . to throw stones.'

'Is that when the Thing appeared?' said Tammy.

Gran nodded.

'We disturbed it with our stones. It must have been growing in the stream for some time, a great leech of a thing, fed by the filth. It rose up out of the Dip and clambered out after us. We ran as fast as we could back to the village but a dreadful storm blew up, with thunder and lightning, and we were forced to shelter in the bakehouse.'

'You must have been terrified,' said William.

'We were,' said Gran. 'And it soon caught up with us and pushed its way into the building. We were cornered there . . . and it reached out for us with horrible tentacles like snakes.'

'Whatever did you do?' said Tammy.

'We threw whatever we could find at it: bags of flour, pans, knives even. But it was the salt that finally stopped it, drying its flesh out before our eyes. We kept covering it with more and more of it until it was dead. But we still didn't feel safe. We were afraid it might come back to life, so we scraped it off the floor and dragged it outside. There was dry wood in the bakehouse. We found matches and lit a bonfire . . . it glowed green, I remember, and filled the air with such a foul stench that it woke half the neighbourhood.'

'Did you get into trouble?' said William.

'We had to clean the bakehouse from top to bottom before we were sent to bed . . . and I was never allowed to play with Edith again.'

Isaac looked round anxiously.

'So why's it back?' he said. 'If you killed it.'

'I think I know why,' I said.

'I'm sure you do,' said Gran. 'But before we talk any more, we must burn these remains. It makes me uneasy to see it again, even like this . . . and who knows what may happen when it rains.'

'She's right,' said Tammy. 'Let's get rid of it.'

'I have matches,' said Gran, feeling in her dressing-gown pocket, 'and we can use some of that garden bark to get it going.'

'But what about the police?' said Tammy.

'I'll offer to settle up with Mr Hoskins, of course, though I'm not sure how I'm going to explain the state of this wall . . . and I hope the police will let a batty old lady off with a caution.'

'But don't you think we should show them the remains?' said Isaac.

'And have them rehydrate the Thing for experiments?' said Gran. 'I think not.'

We made the fire in the field. At first it glowed an evil-smelling green but it eventually subsided to red-hot embers.

'So why *did* it come back,' said Isaac.

'It came back because I lost a gift,' I said. 'A gift from Gran.'

'It was a pretty thing,' said Gran. 'A souvenir. It fitted nicely into the palm of my hand. And I didn't think any harm would come from keeping it.'

'She gave it to me,' I said. 'But I dropped it into the Dip.'

'You mean when you demonstrated the rope drops?' said William.

I nodded.

'It was the seed-case, wasn't it?' said Tammy. 'The furry conker . . . it fell in the Dip and, as soon as it was underwater, it must have started to grow.'

She shivered.

'A furry conker?' said Isaac uncomfortably. 'Where did you get that from then?'

He was looking at Gran.

'I think you might know,' she said, 'because I happened to notice something was missing when we burned the remains. I can't blame you . . . I was tempted myself. It looked like a conker, but so much prettier.'

Across the meadow, we saw a flashing blue light as a police car made its way up Hoskins' drive.

'Perhaps you should own up before they get here,' said Gran.

Isaac drew something from his pocket. It was a small round seed-case about the size of a golf ball and it fitted nicely into the palm of his hand. It was shiny black, but covered with fine green hairs.

'It was on the ground, when we scraped the Thing up,' he said. 'Where its head had been . . . I didn't think it would hurt to keep it.'

'Neither did I, boy,' said Gran as she took it gently from his hand. 'Neither did I.'

And she threw it into the embers.

THE END

THE GENIE OF
THE LAMPPOST
Rachel Dixon

'What is your command, Master?'

Everything's going wrong for Daniel. Bullied
by a rich new boy in town, he's been forced out
of 'The Mob' – the best gang around. Suddenly
no-one wants to know him any more. But then
a very unusual genie fizzles out of an old
lamppost. Will this mysterious visitor solve all
Daniel's problems – or land him in even deèper
trouble?

'Entertaining and brightly written'
THE SCHOOL LIBRARIAN

0 440 863147

THE WITCH'S RING
Rachel Dixon

Trapped by a nasty old witch!

A beautiful ring. A magic word – and Amy
suddenly changes places with a mysterious
lookalike girl. Even worse, she's now the
prisoner of a witch – a horrible, mean, old-
fashioned kind of witch! Can Amy escape before
she is turned into a toad . . . or something
worse?

'A plot which has a real element of originality
. . . children will love all the revolting recipes,
spooky spells and ghastly goings-on'
Weekend Telegraph

0 440 86299X

THE DEMON PIANO
Rachel Dixon

'Bella sat upright, with hands, stiff and white like polished ivory. While her fingers played mechanically, her mouth opened and closed jerkily, as if she were a talking doll . . .'

A ghostly voice rings out in the night, accompanied by a dramatic piano chord. And Bella knows it is *not* just her imagination. Could it perhaps be . . . a warning?

Then Bella's grandmother gives her a piano to play, and Bella finds herself being drawn deeper and deeper into a nightmare. For it is no ordinary piano that she has been given, but one that simply *demands* to be played. And it won't let her stop . . .

'A thrilling, well constructed story told with an excellent balance of fear and fun' *Federation of Children's Book Groups, Pick of the Year*

0 440 862973

ROOM 13
Robert Swindells

The night before her school trip, Fliss has a
terrible nightmare about a dark, sinister house –
a house with a ghastly secret in room thirteen.
Arriving in Whitby, she discovers that the hotel
they will be staying in looks very like the house
in the dream. There is one important difference
– there is no room thirteen.

Or is there? At the stroke of midnight,
something strange happens to the linen
cupboard on the dim landing. Something
strange is happening to Ellie-May Sunderland
too, and Fliss and her friends find themselves
drawn into a desperate bid to save her.

A spooky adventure, full of fun and thrills.

0 440 862272

INSIDE THE WORM
Robert Swindells

The worm was close now. So close Fliss could smell the putrid stench of its breath. Its slavering jaws gaped to engulf her . . .

Everyone in Elsworth knows the local legend about the monstrous worm that once terrorised the village. But it never *really* happened. Or did it? For when Fliss and her friends are chosen to re-enact the legend for the village Festival, something very sinister begins to happen.

Hidden within the framework of the worm costume, the four who are to play the part of the worm dance as one across the ground. And as they sense the exhilaration of awesome power, an intense excitement that tempts them to turn beauty into ugliness, good into evil, Fliss begins to feel real fear. Somehow, the worm itself is returning – with a thousand-year hunger in its belly, and vengeance in its brain . . .

A compelling, fast-paced and spine-chilling new thriller, featuring Fliss and her friends from the award-winning *Room 13*.

0 440 863007

A SELECTED LIST OF TITLES
AVAILABLE FROM YEARLING BOOKS

☐ 862973	**THE DEMON PIANO**	*Rachel Dixon*	£2.99
☐ 86299X	**THE WITCH'S RING**	*Rachel Dixon*	£2.99
☐ 863147	**THE GENIE OF THE LAMPPOST**	*Rachel Dixon*	£2.99
☐ 862779	**SHRUBBERY SKULDUGGERY**	*Rebecca Lisle*	£2.50
☐ 863252	**THE WEATHERSTONE ELEVEN**	*Rebecca Lisle*	£2.99
☐ 862272	**ROOM 13**	*Robert Swindells*	£2.99
☐ 862752	**THE POSTBOX MYSTERY**	*Robert Swindells*	£2.50
☐ 862787	**DRACULA'S CASTLE**	*Robert Swindells*	£2.50
☐ 863139	**HYDRA**	*Robert Swindells*	£2.99
☐ 863163	**THE THOUSAND EYES OF NIGHT**	*Robert Swindells*	£2.99
☐ 863007	**INSIDE THE WORM**	*Robert Swindells*	£2.99
☐ 862019	**THE CREATURE IN THE DARK**	*Robert Westall*	£2.99